Alfred Percy Sinnett

United

A Novel. Vol. 1

Alfred Percy Sinnett

United
A Novel. Vol. 1

ISBN/EAN: 9783337046071

Printed in Europe, USA, Canada, Australia, Japan

Cover: Foto ©Andreas Hilbeck / pixelio.de

More available books at **www.hansebooks.com**

UNITED.

A Novel.

BY

A. P. SINNETT,

AUTHOR OF

"KARMA," "ESOTERIC BUDDHISM," "THE OCCULT WORLD,"

ETC., ETC.

IN TWO VOLUMES.

VOL. I.

LONDON:

GEORGE REDWAY,

YORK STREET, COVENT GARDEN.

1886.

CONTENTS OF VOL. I.

UNITED.

CHAPTER I.

WAKENING TO THE WORLD.

FERRON KINSEYLE had been sorely put out when his wife died. He would not have been rightly described as prostrate with grief; still less so as being heartlessly indifferent. But the principal interests of his life had long been those which gathered round his literary work; and when Mrs. Kinseyle, after ten or twelve years of a quiet existence at Compton Wood, dropped into the grave in a gentle, unobtrusive way, as if it was a matter of course, her husband, roused from his philological researches, realized for the first time that she had been seriously ill. He was very much distressed about it all, though ready to acknowledge, when Bryle, the housekeeper, put it in that way, that Heaven was a better place, at all events for the poor mistress, than Compton Wood. But the recollection of his married life left no painful places in his conscience. "The poor mistress" had been poor by reason of no sins of omission or commission on his part. Bad health had been her worst trouble, and in a little while after that had been finally cured by the translation of the patient to the "better place," just spoken of, the lonely scholar's worst perplexity was developed by the question—what ought to be done about Edith?

Edith was his only daughter—his only child—and at the period referred to had attained the majestic age of six. Her mother, till then, had looked after her in all respects. There had been a nursemaid, of course; but the growth and furniture of Miss Edith's mind had been her mother's care altogether, except, indeed, so far as Miss Edith had partly taken the matter into her own hands—prosecuting independent studies for herself in the library, removing volumes as she wanted them in the early hours of the morning to her own quarters, and leaving

Mr. Kinseyle puzzled sometimes to think what could have become of some book of grave and serious import that he might wish to consult.

Edith's reading was not governed by any frivolous tastes at this stage of her existence, though what the instinct was which prompted her selection of books was a problem Mrs. Kinseyle never attempted to grapple with. The mere fact that the child could read at all, "to amuse herself," so soon, was sufficiently surprising, and not a little creditable to her abilities as a teacher, the admiring mother conceived. For the rest, Edith never consulted anyone as to the course she thought fit to pursue; and Mrs. Kinseyle regarded herself as existing rather to carry out than to constrain her youthful daughter's wishes. And this arrangement had worked so smoothly that the necessity of taking some entirely new departure was exceedingly trying to the widower. He had shrunk from the notion—never very seriously debated with his wife—of having a governess in the house even while Mrs. Kinseyle lived. Compton Wood was not a house of dimensions that would have permitted a life apart

for such an inmate, and the studious philo-
logist was far too shy to bear the prospect of
having a stranger always at his table—a
lady to whom he would have to be polite,
while feeling her presence, from the point of
view of his native reserve, an unutterable
nuisance. Now, however, the thing would
have to be done under conditions much
worse than those which had made it so
unattractive before ; or else Edith would
have to be sent right away somewhere—to
school, or to relations.

Ferron Kinseyle was not a man of large
means, or of large estate ; but he was a
country gentleman, in his way, of eminently
respectable lineage, and the old house,
Compton Wood—a better sort of farmhouse
originally—had been on the family property
for altogether incalculable periods. Most of
the land formerly attached to the name had
gone away, through the female line, to
another rich dynasty, and Ferron Kinseyle,
succeeding from an offshoot parentage, owned
merely a rag of the old Kinseyle estates.
The Miltenhams of Deerbury Park were the
lords of these now ; but they did not make

a residence of Kinseyle Court—two miles across the fields and through its own park from Compton Wood—by reason of having a much more luxurious mansion of their own twenty miles away in another direction.

Kinseyle Court was just kept clean by a man and his wife at the lodge, and shown to visitors who wanted to inspect some old Roman remains preserved around the house. The Miltenhams were too well off to care to . let the place; too respectful to its history, running back to the civil war and further, to neglect it altogether; but too fond of modern comfort to live in it.

The Miltenhams would have taken charge of Edith when her mother died—they were very good friends with the Kinseyles, though their habits of life lay apart—and that seemed the natural arrangement. It was cordially suggested, and at first accepted by the widower; but it was disturbed by an unforeseen embarrassment. Mr. Kinseyle had not up to that time been in the habit of conversing to any great extent with his small daughter. He had no natural affinity for children, and never found anything to say to them. However, when he had in his own mind gratefully accepted Mrs. Miltenham's invitation concerning Edith, he took that young lady on his knee while wandering through the drawing-room and out into the garden one day, soon after the miserable business of the funeral—his usual regular habits of work being thrown out still—and officially informed her of the plans proposed. Then Miss Edith introduced the unforeseen embarrassment referred to.

"But, Papa," she said, "I don't want to go."

Mr. Kinseyle had not looked at the matter from that point of view before. He was too courteous a person to tell the young lady abruptly that nobody talked about her "going"—that the proposal was for her to be sent. Regardless of the risks attending the process when a lady of any age is concerned, he endeavoured to argue the matter.

"My dear Edy, it will be very much the nicest plan for you. There is a little girl about your age at Deerbury Park, and a little boy a year or two younger"—Edy shook her head slightly, but scornfully—"and—and you'll be ever so happy."

"Thank you, Papa, dear; but I would rather stop with you at Compton Wood."

"But, my dear Edy, we should have to have a governess, and that would be a terrible bore for both of us, you know." He did not like to be selfish, so he put the idea that way.

"We'll teach her to behave nicely, Papa," Miss Edith said confidently, and without the least sense of incongruity in thus inverting the natural order of things. And then, as Mr. Kinseyle still held out and pleaded for the Miltenham scheme, Edy brought up all her reserves with the unconscious genius of her sex.

"Oh, Papa!" she cried, more in sorrow than in anger, "you don't mean that you will send me away from you *against my will!*" and with that she melted into tears.

"My dear Edy, my pet, there, don't cry. It really never occurred to me," Mr. Kinseyle frankly confessed, "that you had a will in the matter. It is most curious, the unexpected way family matters may get complicated."

Of course the governess was obtained, and Mr. Kinseyle had to take all the responsibility, in Mrs. Miltenham's eyes, of selfishly choosing an inferior destiny for his daughter, because his own tenderness as a father would not allow him to part with his pet plaything.

He had to face a great deal of acute discomfort when Miss Barkley, the governess Mrs. Miltenham scornfully procured for him, first came on the scene. He did not see, thinking over the matter in advance, how a middle course could be steered between treating the new-comer, on the one hand, as an upper servant—from which attitude he shrank, being very little given to self-assertion—and, on the other, in a way which might entitle her to think he wanted to marry her, which he did not wish to do in the least. But the reality of the situation soon showed itself as less alarming than the prospect. Miss Barkley was a tall, thin spinster, with very prominent teeth, a mild disposition, and a long experience of life. Mr. Kinseyle was relieved. He felt sure that Miss Barkley could not conscientiously expect to be married, and he began to feel more at ease. Perhaps Miss Edith, with her usual influence on all around her, succeeded in teaching her governess how to behave nicely, as she had promised. By degrees, life at Compton Wood resumed something of its old routine. The scholar subsided into his work, and Miss Barkley, impelled by conscience once or twice to inquire whether he wished Edith to do this or that, or leave something else undone, perceived so clearly that he did not wish at all events to be made the arbiter in such transactions, that she chose, practically, the wiser part in her relation with her interesting pupil, and followed that young lady's guidance in all problems of difficulty.

Edith, as the years advanced, consented graciously to pay some visits to Deerbury Park, but she never merged herself altogether in the life of that more brilliant establishment, and grew up in her own quiet home, accepting occasional distractions with cheerful satisfaction when her father, at rare intervals, found reason to spend a month or two in London, but never showing the least impatience of the uneventful and even current of existence at Compton Wood. As time went on, she promoted her father more and more into the rank of companion, drew him out on philosophical questions, and took a friendly interest in his study of comparative Oriental philology, without being impelled herself, however, to follow up these inquiries in detail. As she was troubled by no rude mockery from brothers or sisters, the eccentric development of her mind suffered no offensive shocks, and Mr. Kinseyle's temperament, leading him to accept all the incidents of life as they came, without criticizing them closely unless he was reluctantly compelled to choose some course of action for himself, made him not indifferent to his daughter by any means, but unobservant of her peculiarities as such. Edith was subject in this way to no analytical watchfulness; and though Miss Barkley found strange traits in her character to wonder at sometimes, these were merely oddities, in that good lady's estimation, referable to her old-fashioned bringing up. By the time she was turned fifteen, a natural sense of the fitness of things had taught her to adapt her conversation with Miss Barkley to the governess's understanding, and in this course she was not conscious of any irksome self-restraint, having a plentiful fund of good spirits and gaiety to spend upon the minor affairs of the hour.

One of the most serious difficulties that arose between Miss Barkley and her young charge—or young mistress as she might perhaps have been better described—had to do with an exasperating propensity Miss Edith developed when she was barely out of her childhood, of sitting late in the evening on a big stone near the entrance-gate of Compton Wood, "looking out for the ghost." The house, itself as old as the more stately Court in the neighbourhood, was approached by a long drive with a few trees about—not a regular avenue—with a gate at the end opening into the high-road. Just within the gate were some of the Roman remains scattered about that part of the country in great profusion, and an old labourer belonging to the nearest village, Wexley, declared that when he was a young man he had been frightened nearly out of his wits one night, when going home late from working at Compton Wood, by seeing a white knight on horseback ride in at the gate. He met the figure, he declared, as he was walking in the road himself, and was just close to the gate. He had stepped aside in among the old Roman stones, and the knight had passed him without making any sound as the horse trod; and then the vision had faded away in the direction of the house, before it had got far enough on to have passed out of sight if it had been a veritable man on horseback. The labourer did not tell his story in this connected way, but this was what Edith, who took a great interest in the matter, had made out by prolonged cross-questioning. Investigation of this affair had employed her for many months, as Miss Barkley put every possible impediment in her way, and bitterly reviled an unlucky housemaid from whom she had picked up her original clue. It was a matter of principle with Miss Barkley all the while to repudiate the whole story with the utmost contempt; and it was only on the ground that Miss Edith's head ought not to be stuffed with nonsense that the housemaid was assailed. Edith, on her part, contended that nonsense might be great fun, and that it would be delightful to hunt out

the old labourer and see what he would say.
Bit by bit, in successive walks with Miss
Barkley on summer afternoons, Edith elicited
all that Hodge could tell, though she failed
entirely to get any corroboration of the
tale from any other observer. Then Miss
Barkley had been hoping the uncomfortable
subject might be allowed to drop, when late
in the dusk of one shortening evening in
September, Edith, having been missed and
having been seen strolling down the drive,
was ultimately discovered by the horrified
Miss Barkley sitting alone on the biggest of
the Roman stones at the gate, "looking out
for the ghost."

The vehement though disjointed protests
that Miss Barkley raised on this occasion
culminated in a reference to Mr. Kinseyle.
She had only been able to get Edith away
from the gate—where her own nerves were
too much upset to argue coherently—by
abject entreaties. In the lighted drawing-
room the complicated issues involved were
debated more at length. Miss Barkley ad-
hered to the position that Edith's attempt
was absurd, because ghosts did not exist,

but that she ran the risk of losing her senses
with fright if she should see anything.   It
was clearly wicked to tempt Providence, and
it was perilous, anyhow, in September, to sit
out at night on damp stones, especially when
she knew that her chest was delicate, and
that her poor dear mother had died of con-
sumption.

"And why you're not frightened to death
at the mere thought of such a thing—a child
like you—I can't understand."

"But dear Miss Barkley, what is there to
be frightened of if there is not any white
knight in the case at all?   And that you
say is impossible."

"If you think there's a white knight in the
case," said Miss Barkley, stumbling in despera-
tion on an argument with a certain force,
"that's just as bad."

"I don't know that I think there is," Edith
replied.   "I want to find out."

The governess sought in vain to extort
a promise from Edith that the rash attempt
would not be repeated.   Edith persisted in
surrounding the whole question with an air
of the brightest merriment.   She generously

offered to let Miss Barkley watch for the ghost with her. She proposed that they should harden themselves for the encounter with the white knight by talking about ghosts a good deal in the dark, in their bed-room, and only desisted when Miss Barkley's strained imagination seemed to threaten hysterics.

The reference to Mr. Kinseyle was not made till twice or thrice again the fair Edith had visited her post of observation in the evening. Miss Barkley could neither recon-cile it to her conscience to let this go on, nor venture to hang about the haunted gateway night after night in attendance on her pupil. She knew Mr. Kinseyle would be upset for days if called upon to consider a charge against Edith, and in any way give judgment in the cause ; but the situation was desperate. She was miserably apologetic, but what was to be done about this new and unprecedented freak on Edith's part? " She has slipped out again this evening, and she's alone at that dreadful place at this moment, I'm sure. I'm going after her now, at once, of course ; but I felt bound this time to tell you about it."

Mr. Kinseyle, perplexed and vaguely irritated against poor Miss Barkley, begged her to remain behind, and went in search of Edith himself. He found her on the big stone, and she got up at once and joined him.

"Where's the harm, Papa dear?" she urged, putting her arm through his to walk back down the drive. "I'm wrapped up, as you see, and as warm as a toast. Miss Barkley's so funny about my knight. She's quite frightened."

"But, my pet, young ladies must be taken care of at all times, and especially after dark. If there are no ghosts to be frightened of really—and, as for that, it seems to me very creditable on your part not to be frightened —there are rough men about the world sometimes—robbers, gipsies, and so on."

"But, *Papa!*" said Edith, putting quite a chain of reasoning into the long emphasis on the word, "I stop inside our own gate, and who has ever been robbed about Wexley?"

"Then you see, Edy, imagination is apt to play people tricks when they are expecting to see something supernatural, and—one can't tell—though you're so brave about it to begin with—you might be frightened if you thought you saw something."

" I don't think I should be frightened, because I don't see what harm a ghost would want to do me—if there are ghosts at all. What do you think now, really, about that, Papa ?"

Mr. Kinseyle fenced the question. He was too sincere a person to palm off statements on a child without feeling sure of his own convictions.

" I've not gone into the matter much, Edy. I should lean to the belief that there are not, but if there should be such manifestations in rare cases, I should say we were wisest to let alone what we understand so little about."

" It's very interesting," replied Edith, not entirely convinced by this reasoning.

Miss Barkley met them now in front of the house in a state of nervous agitation. Edith gave her a consolatory kiss, and relieved her, as it were, of all further responsibility in the matter by promising to talk it over with Papa.

" You won't be so cool and composed about it, Edith," Miss Barkley said later on, when they were alone together, " if some evening you do conjure up a dreadful apparition by all this watching."

" Not if it's dreadful, certainly ; but I've confidence in my white knight.   I have not seen him *plainly* yet, but——"

" What ?" cried Miss Barkley, in amazement at the significance of the word thus emphasised.

" But I saw *something* this evening ; something shadowy and vague, you know, but in the shape that would do for a man on horseback.   Soon after that, Papa came up, and I had a feeling that it would be no use to wait any longer this evening, so I came away."

" Well, Edith, your nerves are something I don't understand.   You've destroyed *my* night's rest by merely telling me—what you've just said."

" Dear B., your nerves are in fault though, this time, not mine, surely !"

Edith was contracting a habit about this time of calling her governess " B." as a friendly abbreviation of her full name, which, used without the prefix, that grew troublesome in constant repetition, would have put her on too humble a level.

The young lady's visits to the Miltenhams, both at Deerbury Park and in London, gave her, as time went on, the *savoir vivre* befitting her natural station, without quenching her taste for the quiet life of her own home, where she fed her mind by enterprising excursions through realms of literature where B. found herself hopelessly unable to follow, and where her beauty expanded without involving her in the excitement it might have set in motion round her had she approached seventeen in the midst of an ebb and flow of society. She was slight but very gracefully developed in figure, *petite* rather than otherwise as to height, but with a very upright carriage and a self-confident composure of manner that gave an almost comic touch of stateliness to her small proportions, and her fair though richly tinted complexion, sweetly delicate features, large blue eyes, and golden hair, invested her with undeniable claims to admiration.

Her love of the quiet seclusion of Compton Wood was born of no shrinking timidity of nature, still less of any morose dislike of her fellow creatures. The sunny brightness of her own temperament gilded the old house with all the gaiety she required. Inheriting, though transmuting to a brighter phase, some of her father's attributes, she took things as they came, and never stopped to weigh and consider circumstances round her in a discontented or critical mood. Compton Wood was her home, so at Compton Wood she habitually abided; always treating her visits to the Miltenhams as such—to be enjoyed, certainly, while they lasted, but to terminate in due season, as a matter of course.

CHAPTER II.

THE FIRST MEETING.

THE library at Kinseyle Court wooed her away, two or three years later, from the old Roman stones at the gate, where she had first developed her inclination for ghostly watching. Miss Barkley was hardly the gainer by the change, however, for the half deserted old house was not a " canny " habitation after dusk for people nervous about such fancies, and it was sometimes difficult to draw Edith away, as evening approached, if she was seized with an inclination to sit on in the old library, or in the "Countess's Study" attached; —a room reached up two or three steps from the larger chamber, and bearing that traditional name by virtue, as Edith discovered for herself in the course of her reading, of certain incidents connected with the past history of the family.

The Countess in question had been a daughter of the Kinseyle house, who returned home on her husband's death, during the troubles of the civil war. The luckless lady had resided for a long time almost alone at Kinseyle Court, the representative of the family at the time being a younger brother, away on his travels. Then, when he came home in due season with a wife, the Countess removed to a neighbouring house of her own —not very plainly identified in the old family memoirs from which Edith gleaned these particulars, but suspected by her to be Compton Wood—keeping only one room at Kinseyle Court, the aforesaid " study."

These comparatively trifling incidents had been recorded by a scholarly Kinseyle, of a literary turn, belonging to the following generation, because of the strange reports concerning the " Countess's Study," which he found current in his time, and set down with grave simplicity. The lady was alleged to have practised some variety of the " black art," and strange voices had been heard by servants from the grounds outside her windows when she was known to be alone inside. After her death, her wraith had been seen at these same windows in the moonlight; and though the room was shut up and put to no ordinary uses by her immediate successors at the Court, it would sometimes be seen from afar lighted up with a steady white light, that suggested no alarm of fire, but even more acute, if more fantastic, terrors connected with the supernatural.

Since those days the room had been turned to ordinary uses by later generations of Kinseyles; but still it retained the old name, and remained furnished as a study or writing-room, though refitted and modernized, of course, more than once since the remote epoch in which it had served the needs of the mysterious Countess.

It pleased Edith to sit there in an old green Utrecht velvet arm-chair that stood by the table, or in one of the deep window-seats that looked out upon the park, and dream of the bygone time, or take some books up there from the library below, gathered at random from the shelves, and dive into them in the spirit of an explorer travelling through an unknown country. Perhaps these desultory studies left no particular fruits of culture in her mind, but they interested her for the time; and Miss Barkley had learned long before the period at which Edith took to frequenting Kinseyle Court that her duties did *not* include the exercise of any censorship over the young lady's literary taste. Miss Barkley's anxiety in the matter had to do, not so much with the direction this took, as with the unseemly hours at which Edith persisted in gratifying it.

Dinner was an early ceremony at Compton Wood, for Mr. Kinseyle liked an evening that was something more than the ragged end of dessert, and, regardless of convention, took his principal meal at five o'clock. This left the ladies with so much daylight on their hands afterwards in the summer and autumn, that Edith was enabled to march her reluctant chaperone across the fields, sometimes in the evening for an eerie visit to the Countess's Study in the dusk. Miss Barkley would put impediments in the way as far as she could, preferring a simpler and more domestic routine; but Edith met all difficulties with her usual promptitude and determination. Squires could see them home if they were tempted to stay too late. Squires, with his wife, constituted the care-taking establishment of Kinseyle Court, and resided at the lodge. Both by reason of orders from his regular superiors at Deerbury Park, and by virtue of his ready inclination to serve the young lady's caprices, he regarded her in all respects as having authority at the Court, and loyally put aside Miss Barkley's suggestion when the practice first arose—that it was a tax on his time to perform escort duty in the evening.

"I was quite sure Squires would be glad to be of use to me," Edith said graciously, with the air of a young queen conferring a favour in accepting her subject's homage; and the veteran retainer besought her "never to be within sending for Squires," whatsoever it might be that was wanted.

Of course Edith joyously recounted to Miss Barkley all the tales she could find in the old family memoir above mentioned which bore reference to spectral phenomena associated with the Countess's Study.

Miss Barkley scoffed—and shivered a little in secret at times—but would not give in to

Edith's whim so far as to recognise the danger of seeing the ghost as an objection attending evening visits to the Court. Indeed, there had been no pretence of any ghost in the case for several hundred years. It was too absurd of Edith to be making believe to expect one in this case.

"Then you *do* feel that in the other case Hodge's story about the White Knight is important?" Miss Edith maliciously urged in reply.

But "B." would only stand to her guns during the day time in safe places. In serious emergencies after sunset, she would fall back upon honest confessions of feeling fidgety and plaintive entreaties to be taken home. Then Edith would compromise matters, and promise to join her at the lodge in half an hour if left at peace and undisturbed in her dear old library or in the study, as the case might be, for the pleasant interval between the lights.

"It is quite unaccountable how Miss Edith can dare to stop alone in those old rooms, when it's getting dark like this," Miss Barkley exclaimed, in conversation with Mrs. Squires at the lodge one evening under circumstances of this kind. "It isn't as if she was a masculine sort of girl. She isn't the least of a tomboy, but she actually likes to be alone in places that would make anybody else nervous with all sorts of foolish fancies."

"Bless your soul, m'm, it's all right," put in Mr. Squires from the little garden outside. Long familiarity with the Court, and its clean bill of health in regard to such matters as those Miss Barkley hinted at, made the custodian of the place disinclined to admit that anyone could incur peril there. "There ain't aught to be a-feared of at Kinseyle Court, night time or day."

"Of course I didn't say there was really," replied Miss Barkley, with a little asperity; "only for a girl like Miss Edith, one might expect that she would have been timid. And it is getting so late this evening. It's past the time she said she would join me here."

Miss Barkley stepped out into the road and looked up the avenue, but it was already impossible to see far through the thick shade of the trees, and a slight turn in the road concealed the house itself from view from the lodge, though the actual distance was inconsiderable. No comforting vision of the creamy white dress in which Edith's graceful figure was robed that day was to be discerned, and Miss Barkley had to go back and bring her patience to bear upon the trying situation. Mrs. Squires's gossip was not altogether to be despised by a resident at so quiet a house as Compton Wood, as she commanded news through Thracebridge, whence she drew her supplies, relating to a tract of country which lay beyond the jurisdiction of Wexley, the village with which Miss Barkley's household was in relations. Still, to be five-and-twenty minutes late in keeping an appointment which is only entitled to deal with a total period of half an hour, is to push unpunctuality too far. When Miss Barkley realized that she had been kept waiting so long, she was half indignant and half alarmed.

" What *can* be keeping her so long? It's actually getting dark! *Would* Mr. Squires mind going up to the house and asking her if she isn't coming?"

" I'll go and wait for her, m'm, if you

like, at the door; but I wouldn't like to go in for to disturb her if she sees fit for to stop," said Squires, after some consideration of the problem. "If you come along. too, m'm, you can go in and see if she's ready."

Miss Barkley hated poking about the old house after dark; and the situation was not made any better that evening by the fact that a full moon was rising.

"Miss Edith asked me to wait for her at the lodge," she answered, suddenly reverting to the theory that Miss Edith's will had to be obeyed to the letter.

Squires could not have analysed the fallacy involved in her position, as coupled with her wish to disturb the young lady vicariously, but was setting out up the drive, when the sudden barking of a black and tan retainer of the lodge household drew attention to two gentlemen who had come along the public road and were now pausing at the gate. Squires turned back and went to interview them.

"This is Kinseyle Court, isn't it?" said the taller of the two, leaning on the low iron gate that swung across the entrance to the drive, and holding out half-a-crown to Squires as he approached. The gardener accepted the peace-offering with easy grace, and answered with the friendly cheerfulness that seemed due to an acquaintance so pleasantly begun. He opened the smaller side-gate as he spoke, and the visitors came in.

" There's no family living here, I understand ?"

" *No—o*, sir, not for many a long day."

" Ah ! We had a fancy to look at the place, which visitors are permitted to see, I believe ?"

" Yes, sir ; certainly."

" But I'm afraid it's too late this evening. We did not quite know how long it would take us to walk out here from Thracebridge."

The visitors seemed undecided, none the less, and strolled in a few steps beside Mr. Squires.

" Well, it is a bit late, sir, to see anything to-night, sir. Any time in the *day* you might be passing——"

" 'M—yes. By-the-bye, it might be a good thing perhaps to rest a little before we return. Now, if you can give us chairs here in your garden for ten minutes, that would be very obliging of you."

The speaker hardly looked like a person who would be prostrate with fatigue as the result of a walk from Thracebridge. He was a young man of eight-and-twenty or thirty, well made, with a vigorous athletic physique, a short-cut, brown beard, and moustache—clearly a gentleman by all external signs of dress and manner; and a finer observer than Mr. Squires might have been struck by the fact that his demand for the means of resting was not given out in the manner of a wearied wayfarer, but as if by a sudden happy inspiration. At any rate, the loan of a couple of chairs for ten minutes was well within the credit established by the half-crown, so Squires agreed cordially, and the strangers followed him into the little front-garden of the lodge. Then for the first time perceiving Mrs. Squires and Miss Barkley, who stood just outside the threshold, they lifted their hats to Miss Barkley, and looked a little discomfited.

"I beg your pardon. I hope we are not in your way. We were going to rest for a little after a short walk—at least, after what I ought to call a long walk, if I feel tired."

Miss Barkley bowed, muttering a few words of vague courtesy ; and Mr. Squires bade his wife get the gentlemen chairs. The shorter and slighter of the two—perhaps not the younger, though wearing no hair about his face beyond a slight fringe of light brown moustache; rather colourless as to complexion, but with a small. pale face of great intelligence, made all the more striking by large, dark eyes of piercing expression—said nothing, and seemed to be merely following the guidance of his friend. The friend went on talking—rather as though to combat a slight feeling of embarrassment than from having any purpose in what he said, though all the while speaking in a tone that implied finished breeding.

"Stupid of us to have come out so late. We had a wish to see this place, and stopped here on our way north. We ought to have stayed at the inn, and to have come out here in the morning."

"You are connected with the Kinseyle family, perhaps," Miss Barkley said.

"No, not at all. My people are from Gloucestershire; but I was particularly asked to look at Kinseyle Court by someone interested in the place. Not that there's any particular reason for it; it's only a fancy."

Miss Barkley's curiosity was beginning to assert itself about the stranger. Mrs. Squires now came out with the chairs; but the visitors remained standing, the talkative one willingly entering into conversation with Miss Barkley, as she remarked that Kinseyle Court was not much of a show place. It was only interesting for the sake of a few antiquities, and for its age and history.

"The people the place belongs to now never come here, then?"

"The Miltenhams? No; they live at Deerbury Park. The Court would have to be almost rebuilt, I believe, to suit them."

"And do not any members of the family come here? I thought I had been told something to that effect—about some of them having a special affection for the house."

"Oh dear no; they are quite a different kind of people to that. But, Squires, don't you think you had better be going up to the

house to see after Miss Edith? I really am
getting uneasy."

The stranger caught with interest at this
remark, as Squires prepared to do as he was
asked, returning first to shut the side-gate
into the road.

"Then there are some people staying at
the Court at present, do I understand,
though not any of the family you mentioned?"

"Not staying there; only my pupil, Miss
Kinseyle, has been looking over some books
in the library this afternoon, and I am waiting
to go home with her." Miss Barkley always
liked to give as well as to receive gossip.
"Perhaps you are acquainted with Mr.
Kinseyle of Compton Wood?"

"I have not that pleasure, though I should
value it very highly. Pardon me if I seem
very obtrusive and impertinent. My name
is Ferrars—George Ferrars—and my sister,
Mrs. Malcolm, must be acquainted, I fancy,
with the young lady you have just spoken of.
She especially asked me to go and look at
Kinseyle Court, to tell her something about
it she was curious to know. And now, I

think, as our friend the lodge-keeper seems to be going up to the house, I should like to walk up the avenue with him and glance at the outside, at all events—that may suffice for my purpose."

Hereupon, Miss Barkley declared that she would go also; her instinctive sense of duty as chaperone triumphing over her reluctance to return to the twilight shadows of the Court. As they all went up the avenue, she improved the opportunity for getting at the origin of Mr. Ferrars's curiosity.

" If you tell me what it is you want to know about the Court, I might be able to help you. I have lived a long while with Miss Kinseyle, and am often here."

" Ah—then Miss Kinseyle is doubtless the young lady I was referring to, who has an affection for the house, and is in some way specially identified with it. It is very strange."

" Why should it be strange? Miss Kinseyle is in one way the last representative of the old family."

" I beg your pardon again. My questions must seem rather crazy, even if you are good enough to credit me with not being impertinent. How can I explain? Tell me; are you much in the way of hearing about queer coincidences, strange mental impressions, you know—clairvoyance and that sort of thing?"

"Oh, I dislike all that sort of thing *extremely.* I hear a great deal too much of it from Miss Kinseyle as it is, and I do not believe anything about it."

"But the young lady does, it would seem. That makes the matter all the more curious. Now, I will make a full confession, Miss —— at least; ah, I beg your pardon, I forgot that I had not been properly introduced."

Miss Barkley mentioned her name. Mr. Ferrars had a straightforward, confident manner that she would have been unable to resist even if she had had any motive for so doing.

"You see," he went on, "my sister, Mrs. Malcolm has a good deal to do with that sort of thing I was just speaking of, clairvoyance and what not. Personally, I am like you, you know, I haven't anything to do

with it to speak of. But my sister is
different. And she has got an impression—
I can't tell you how she has got it—that she
very much wants to know a young lady who
is somehow specially connected with an old
house called Kinseyle Court. I had not
even got the name quite right till to-day.
She spelt it wrong. She did not know
the young lady's name, nor where the house
was situated, except that it was somewhere
about England. I have had a lot of trouble
about it with county directories, but now it
would seem that I have got upon what she
wants to know. And that is all that con-
cerns me. Of course, I should not be
impertinent enough to present myself to the
young lady, and should have nothing to say
to her if I did. But my sister knows everybody in London, and can easily get a proper
introduction to anybody she wants to know,
when once she knows who it is she wants to
know, don't you know. The whole situation
seems a little mixed, but it is very simple,
really."

Miss Barkley wondered and marvelled
over the strange coincidence, and did not

know whether it would be necessary to tell Miss Kinseyle anything about it; but admitted that there could be nothing to prevent Mrs. Malcolm seeking to make the acquaintance of the Kinseyle family through any of the usual channels of society.

When they got up to the house, she led the way round the front to the corner in which the library was situated, and called out to her pupil, but without getting any answer. The windows were too high from the ground to be looked into from the outside. This end of the building was now bathed in the light of the moon, which poured an almost level radiance across an open space that should have been a flower garden, and the twilight—of which, indeed, but little now survived—was entirely overcome by the whiter illumination. The tall lattice windows shone steadily in the moonlight, but no answering voice came from them, nor did any sign of Edith appear there.

" What can she be about ?" Miss Barkley exclaimed in much vexation. " I must go in and see. Really, it is the strangest taste that can make her stop here so late."

"If I can be the slightest use, pray command me. Would you wish me to wait here, or to accompany you?"

"Really, I hardly know. Please just come into the hall, and then I will go in search of Miss Kinseyle, while you wait there. Goodness! it's quite dark in here." They had penetrated to the hall by this time, and Miss Barkley was advancing to the left with a beating heart, and towards the library door, dimly discernible up a few stairs and beyond a broad landing, lighted, though faintly just then, from above. As Miss Barkley opened the big door, light seemed to come freely from the room by reason of the moon shining brilliantly through the large windows at the end.

"Edith!" she cried in the same impatient tone as before, as she opened the door, and then again, '*Edith!*' in a wilder tone of alarm—almost a scream—as she stepped into the room. "What is the matter, in Heaven's name!"

Her cry of terror overbore the instructions she had given to her escort to remain in the hall. Both young men sprang up the half-dozen stairs in a moment, and followed her into the library.

Edith was half kneeling, half lying prostrate on the floor, her creamy white dress shining as though luminous in the moonbeams, her hands clasped together, stretched before her and resting on a footstool, and her face turned upwards towards the side door, near the window end of the room, which led into the Countess's Study. She was in no faint, however, as Miss Barkley had supposed at the first glance. As the governess rushed forward towards her she rose on to her knees, motioning Miss Barkley back with her left hand, and then got up entirely, still gazing into the inner room.

"Oh, why did you disturb us?" she said in a dreamy tone, advancing towards the open door and standing with her right hand upon the side of the entrance.

"What do you mean by ' us,' Edith?" Miss Barkley replied piteously, with tears of nervous excitement in her voice. "Is anything the matter? You speak in such a strange way."

"The matter! Oh no!"—though Miss

Kinseyle's manner was dreamy it was not sad or oppressed : rapt, rather, and ecstatic. " I feel as if I had been in Heaven. But now she has gone."

She turned towards Miss Barkley, and for the first time saw Ferrars and his companion in the background, standing near the door of the library.

" Who is with you ?"

" Only two gentlemen who came to my assistance. I was frightened about you. But you will come away, dear, now, won't you ? You're not feeling ill, are you ? You didn't faint ?"

Miss Kinseyle was too deeply absorbed still by the impressions she had been going through to answer promptly to Miss Barkley's questions. Meanwhile Ferrars began to feel *de trop*.

" I came up the stairs because you cried out and seemed frightened," he said to Miss Barkley. " I will wait for you in the hall, as you told me," and with that he retired.

His companion, however, seemed more reluctant to move, and half turning as if to follow Ferrars, remained in the shadow of the doorway intently watching Miss Kinseyle, who was now seated on the stool she had been leaning across when they came in. Miss Barkley was kneeling beside her.

" Dear B., I'm quite well, only a little excited. A glass of water would be refreshing. Can you get me one, do you think ?"

" Yes, dear, I'll try."

Miss Barkley was getting up, when the stranger interposed.

" May I be of service ? Pray remain with the young lady, and let me go in search of the water."

" Oh, thank you—but you won't know where to get it."

" The keeper will show me."

He went off quickly on his errand.

" Who is it, B. ? He has a pleasant voice."

" They are two gentlemen who came to see the Court. One of them has been talking to me as we came up the drive. There is something queer about it. I will tell you as we go home ; but I'm so flurried and frightened—I don't know why. I do so wish we were back home."

" Poor B.," said Miss Kinseyle in a soothing, protecting tone. " Don't be alarmed ; it's an angel I have seen, not a ghost. I feel as if I could hardly tear myself away. Let me first stand a few moments where *she* has been standing," and she went up the two steps, remaining just within the door of the study. "Oh, B. dear, I have had such a glorious vision! The beautiful angel has been here, just where I am standing, talking to me for I don't know how long, filling my mind with such rapture, I can't describe it to you. I feel that still. I have been lifted up out of myself—I can't bear to come down again."

"My dear Edith, perhaps you have been dreaming. But you are not frightened, at any rate, that's one good thing."

"Frightened!" Miss Kinseyle answered, with a dreamy emphasis on the word that implied a wealth of feelings of quite an opposite kind; and then, turning inwards towards the smaller room, she stretched out her hands and murmured in a low voice, as though addressing some invisible presence, "Good-night, dearest—good-bye till I see you again, and may that be soon."

Then she came down into the library, and put her hand on Miss Barkley's arm, feeling her tremble, and divining her nervous agitation.

"My poor B., don't you be frightened. There is nothing to be frightened about, I assure you. Sit down and recover yourself."

"I'm glad we are not quite alone here. It was really most providential those gentlemen coming up just when they did. I don't think there's any doubt about their really being gentlemen. The one I was talking to—the other one—says his people belong to Gloucestershire. His name is Ferrars."

"How dreadfully prosaic; and I suppose the other one has got some stupid name too, and 'people' in another county. I like people to be *themselves*, whoever they are, and not mere family appendages of somebody else."

"I don't know what the other one's name is——" Miss Barkley began, but at that moment he came back with the water.

"I hope this will refresh you," he said, bowing as he presented it.

Now that his hat was off, the most remarkable feature of his face was seen to be a broad high forehead, showing great intellectual power, surmounted by closely-cut and not very thick light brown hair, parted in the middle. As he stood in the full and vivid moonlight, presenting the glass of water, the pallor of his complexion and the depth of his large dark eyes were both intensified ; and Miss Kinseyle was conscious of a thrill of excitement she could hardly account for as he looked at her.

" You only feel, as it were, disinclined to move—neither weak nor alarmed ?" he said in a tone of confident inquiry.

" That is just it," she replied. " I can't tear myself away, though I suppose I ought."

" Drink a little of the water, and you will feel light and active again."

" You have not put anything in it ? I hate brandy and things of that sort."

" It is pure water, with only a little magic in it—for you, at this moment. And it will not be at war with your vision."

Vaguely wondering at the confident tone in which he spoke and seemed to understand her, but impelled to feel very trustful, Miss Kinseyle drank some of the water, looking at him all the while—fascinated, as it were, by the keen look he bent upon her, and emancipated from the formalities of life by the singular conditions of the scene. She got up when she had returned him the glass of water, and they all went out of the library at once, and into the open air, as if that had been previously arranged. She said nothing about feeling stronger, but with animated interest, as they went, asked:

"What do you know about my vision?"

"Nothing concerning it," he said, "which may be private to yourself. Nothing concerning it which is definite at all; but I can see its reflection on your face, and it must have been a beautiful vision, and a noble one, to have left such traces."

"But what do such things mean? Can you tell me anything about them? Do you know?"

"About such things one may know just a little more than one's neighbour, and yet be only overwhelmed with a sense that we only know about their faintest fringes. If I said I knew nothing, I should mislead you. If I said I knew much, I should seem false to my own consciousness."

They were all standing in the open space before the house. Miss Barkley, feeling the strain of the situation to be relaxing, began to come again under the dominion of her sense of duty as chaperone.

"Squires will see to the hall door, dear," she said, "and follow us immediately. I'm sure we have to thank these gentlemen most warmly for coming to our assistance; but now I think of it, we must say good evening, and hurry home."

"Yes, we will walk on. We are all going the same way to the gate," said Miss Kinseyle, with the calm composure ensuing from her inner consciousness that her will, once defined plainly, was never practically disputed. She moved forward with her new friend by her side, and Miss Barkley followed them, closely attended by Mr. Ferrars.

"I dare say," Miss Kinseyle went on, "that what you call very little knowledge would seem a great deal to me. I know nothing. I understand nothing about what I see. I can only gaze and feel enraptured, and long to know more. And none of my people seem to understand me."

" You know more by the light of your own great gifts, evidently, than most of us who study these things can find out in a lifetime. It is so difficult to explain. We, who are students of the occult mysteries of nature—for I may at any rate call myself a student of these—spend our time groping through intricate theories for the means of compassing such visions as those that seem to come to you by nature. If I were privileged to be in any sense your teacher, it would only be in the beginning that I should be able to teach. I could only teach you to understand the priceless value of your own powers, and then it would be my part to learn of and through you."

" But you know I do not have such an experience as that I have had to-day at all often. I never had quite *such* a one before. Is it so rare for people to have visions of any sort? It has seemed to me sometimes as if the people round me must be the exceptional people in *not* seeing things sometimes."

" I understand your feeling; but it is a mistake, though natural to you. There are just enough of the highly endowed creatures of your kind in the world to show us, who are students of Nature's mysteries, that you are dealing with realities, though these may only occasionally be observed. You are certainly not all self-deceived, nor imposing on the rest of the world, to the same effect, without any concert among yourselves."

"I am sure I never exaggerate anything, and yet people don't seem quite to believe what I tell them about impressions I have. It is so strange to feel quite sure you have seen so and so, whatever it may be, and then to have people look incredulous or pretend you were dreaming, when you know quite well you were wide awake."

"That is one of the little penalties of your superiority. But, sooner or later, you will be sure to meet many people who will understand you."

"You seem to be the first I have met yet; and you do not make me understand myself altogether."

"Have patience a little while longer— the rest will come,—a fuller comprehension of yourself, and of a great deal beyond. What is the use of attempting to go into so vast a

subject with so little time at my command.
I am *sure* you will not have to wait long for
the most helpful guidance and instruction
you can need."

" Where will it be that I shall meet people
who can help me ? Will it be with my
cousins, the Miltenhams ? That is my only
outlet into society. Do you know them ?"

" No; but that is my fault. I lead a very
retired life. It is necessary that I should for
many reasons."

" Can I do nothing to seek help ? I feel as
if you know much more than you say—more
even about me, though we are strangers—so
far."

He made no immediate reply.

Miss Kinseyle could feel rather than see, in
the darkness of the avenue, that he was
grave and sad, and in no way responsive to
what was almost an invitation on her part to
a more intimate acquaintance.

Presently he said, with some flavour of
constraint in his voice :

" Later on, if I can be of any use to you,
you will have easy means of commanding
my services. I hope, for your sake, you

will find others at your disposal better worth having. I rarely step outside a very narrow path in life."

The young lady felt a little mortified and rebuffed, and they walked on for a while in silence.

" My counsel," he resumed, after this interval, and the earnest tone in which he spoke, and its sadness, which now seemed to overshadow its constraint, changed her feeling of annoyance into one of undefined sympathy, " can only be just of transitory service for the moment—pending better. But for the moment I will presume to advise. Do not waste your confidence, as regards your own inner experiences, on people, however good and entitled to your affection in other ways, who take up that attitude you spoke of, of incredulity about them. You, evidently, have gifts which mark you out as one of a select few on this earth. You will assuredly meet your proper companions, as regards your higher spiritual life, as time goes on. Be patient, meanwhile, and watchful ; treasuring up your higher experiences, and leading two lives for the moment—one outer, and the other inner; but remembering that the inner is really by far the more important of the two. Do not let the other crush it. For all of us, if we could only realize it, the spiritual life is the more important; but only a few of us have the immense privilege you enjoy of being already able to secure that as a reality. That is the first great lesson for you to learn; but I think you have learned so much already. Forgive me, however, for presuming to preach; your own intuitions will show you all this a thousand times more forcibly than I can."

"But, indeed, I am asking you to preach as you call it. All you say is full of interest, and seems to clear things up for me more than I can tell you. You seem to wake up a consciousness of my own, that I did not rightly understand before. I do lead the double life you speak of, and it has fretted me hitherto; but now I understand the right attitude of mind about it."

They were nearing the gate now, but a sudden thought crossed Edith's fancy.

"How was it we came away from the

library so suddenly? I meant to have lingered on."

"You felt fresher and more active after you had drunk the water."

"But now I remember; what did you mean by saying there was a little magic in it?"

"You are very, very sensitive. It was merely my desire to make you feel stronger and better. Your vital energy had been a little impaired by your excitement."

"But how was your desire communicated to me? I do feel strong and energetic. I did not notice it before——"

The others closed up on them now, however, as they came opposite the lodge.

Mr. Squires had overtaken them, and Miss Barkley called to him to accompany them home. She was getting nervous about the prolonged interview with strangers, and anxious to part company, in a way which Mr. Ferrars perceived, not without internal amusement. She would have parted simply with gracious words and thanks and bows; but Edith held out her hand, first to Mr. Ferrars sa they all stood together by the gate, and

then to her companion. With the queenlike
and composed dignity which sat so naturally
on her, though so quaintly in contrast with her
small slight figure, she said, as she did so :

" I should be glad to know to whom I am
indebted for so much interesting conversation ?"

" Allow me," said Ferrars, lifting his hat,
" to present my friend—' Mr. Sidney Marston.' "

They all bowed, with a sudden access of
formality, and the ladies turned up the road,
followed by Squires, while the strangers
retreated in the opposite direction towards
Thracebridge.

CHAPTER III.

MARSTON, on whose slight physique the double walk, or some other influences, had told more than on his companion, went to his room to lie down with a book and a pipe soon after the apology for a dinner with which the village inn they were staying at supplied them ; and Ferrars spent the evening writing to his sister a report of his proceedings, infused with much eulogy of the skill he had shown in following up her very inadequate clue.

" You tell me," he wrote, " that somewhere about England there is a young lady you want me to find for you, and you do not know her name, nor appearance, nor who she belongs to. You say, you fancy she must live at a place called Kinsale Court, probably situated in the British Islands. There isn't any such place in existence, and there is no young lady living there ; but all the same, I have found you the young lady you want, and her name is Edith Kinseyle, and she is the daughter of a man named Ferron Kinseyle, who lives at Compton Wood, in Midhamptonshire. She must be your young lady, for she haunts the old house of her family, Kinseyle—not Kinsale—Court, and is evidently given to having ecstatic visions, quite in your line. How have I found her out ? By the exercise of superlative genius. How am I rewarded for my devotion to your behests ? By spending the evening in a den of a village inn—poor dear Sidney Marston, who came with me to bear me company, being seedy, and having gone to bed—writing, with a bad pen, on worse paper, by the light of a wretched couple of candles, on an absurd bedroom dressing-table ; when, if I had not come here, to serve a tyrannical sister, I should have been actually sitting at dinner, at this moment, beside Terra Fildare at Oatfield.

"Perhaps that would not necessarily have been heaven for me, you will argue—and I

freely grant that it might have been an
arrangement with a spice of the other place,
if Terra had been in a bad mood. But even
if I have not finally conquered my Queen
yet, I must be vigorously prosecuting the
war, or life is unendurable. You resent the
notion, do you not, that even a Terra Fildare
should play fast and loose with your excel-
lent brother. But it does not seem to me
strange that such a princess should deliberate
awhile before surrendering so grand a prize
as herself to the first man who comes along
and says, ' Please come and be my property
for the rest of your life.' The oddity of the
situation is merely in the confidence there is
between you and me ; but then we are not
like other brothers and sisters. We are all
in all to each other, and it is merely a
mystery of love that I can be filled in every
pore with passionate enthusiasm for Terra,
and yet be entirely devoted to you, as I
always have been since life gave me any
memory of my emotions, and always must
be to the end. And you are so penetrating
in your comprehension of this, that you can
love Terra with me, and only reserve your-

self the right of hating her if she decides to do without me.

"There is the only mistake you make—though so pardonable in you. She will be quite within her right either way, and I shall love her either way—to my sorrow or my joy, as she may settle things; and I do not see how it is conceivable that, in that way, I can ever love another woman. In talking over this with you we are apt to get desultory, so I think I have not wasted this evening altogether in putting the idea into accurate words."

Ferrars posted his letter the following morning on his way to the railway station, where the two friends parted, Mr. Marston returning to London, Ferrars going on North. Mr. Squires was thus disappointed of the other half-crown he counted on from the gentlemen who had been so eager to see Kinseyle Court. It had not occurred to Ferrars the previous evening to explain that having achieved success in the final purpose with which he had come to see the Court, it would be unnecessary for him to return the next day. So Squires looked out for him and even mentioned that he was still expecting the two gentlemen, when Edith and Miss Barkley came across, the day after the young lady's vision in the library. This midday visit was a sort of compromise. Miss Kinseyle had proposed that they should again go after dinner, but Miss Barkley had suffered much over the prospect. Did Edith wish to drive herself mad, or sell herself to the Evil One, or give a handle to superstition, by letting herself fancy she had made acquaintance with a ghost, when everybody knew perfectly well that Kinseyle Court was quite free of any nuisance of the kind, so far? It would be Edith who would be responsible for spoiling the character of the house, if she went about deliberately encouraging ghosts to come there; and would it not be only right at all events to discuss the whole subject with her father? On that point Miss Barkley scored. Edith could not deny that this would be a proper course to pursue, but there was no hurry. She would like to make quite sure of some things first before talking to Papa.

" My dear Edith, what things ?" Miss

Barkley apprehended that the young lady contemplated some fresh reference to the ghost.

"Some things about the history of the family, I mean. I can't remember everything *She* said to me. I can't remember a quarter of it, and I am longing to see her again. But for the moment what I want is to look up something in the Kinseyle Annals."

"We need not wait till the gray of the evening for that, at all events," Miss Barkley pointed out. "Why not go over this morning?"

On reflection Edith agreed, and it was only when she remarked later, as they were walking across the fields, that very likely Mr. Ferrars and Mr. Marston would be at the Court during the morning, that Miss Barkley perceived she had swayed over from Scylla to Charybdis. To avoid the ghost she had steered her pupil into the companionship of strange gentlemen of a somewhat obtrusive temperament—possibly undesirable admirers in disguise. But, as already stated, the anxiety she felt on this subject was thrown away.

Neither Mr. Ferrars nor his friend turned up at all, and—without avowing it to herself even, still less to Miss Barkley— Edith perhaps shared, for different reasons, the regret and disapproval Mr. Squires frankly expressed.

" I don't see what call he had to make out he was in such a hurry to see the Court. I don't understand that chap," said the lodge-keeper, vaguely suspicious, when the ladies bade him good-bye in the afternoon.

Ferrars, meanwhile, was speeding on his way North towards the country house near the Lakes, at which he was looking forward to meeting the lady, of whom he had written to his sister. Oatfield was the pleasant seat of a county magnate, who in his time had represented his Sovereign abroad on one or two ornamental occasions—Sir James Margreave. Ferrars—himself in the early stages of the diplomatic career—had served under Sir James, and had been his guest at Oatfield since then, on two or three occasions, when at home on leave. Terra Fildare was a niece of the baronet, daughter of a colonel in the service of the Government of India,

who had married his sister, since dead. She
had no money to speak of, but a splendid
physique—the head and bust of a Roman
Empress—tawny hair, cut short, for a whim
of the wearer, but massive and abundant and
curling low over her forehead ; a glowing
complexion, a majestic figure—the poses of
which, however, were quite unstudied, for
her nature was impulsive and her vitality
too vigorous to be compatible with any
queenly langour—and an almost unruly love
of outdoor activity in all the forms accessible
to her as a girl. A hankering after some
that were thus inaccessible made her sometimes impatient of her sex. She had spent
some years of early girlhood with her father
in India ; had shot a tiger from an elephant's
howdah—an exploit organized for her by a
Spanish Count, who had been travelling
through the North-west Provinces at the
time, and the fame of which spread far too
widely for her pleasure and comfort or her
father's approval ; and had soon after this
been sent home, for fear she should fall a
victim in her turn to some one or other of a
crowd of young officers at the station where

Colonel Fildare found himself fixed for a year or two at least. Lady Margreave had given her a long invitation, privately promising the Colonel to dispose of the young lady to better advantage than amongst the enamoured subalterns at Chuckapore.

Lady Margreave was the one other person besides his sister to whom Ferrars had confided the fact that he had invested his prospects of happiness in the uncertain issue of the siege he had laid to Terra Fildare's heart. She had neither favoured nor opposed his views. At first she had counted on a rather brilliant settlement for her splendid niece. Her own family of sons left her ambition as a matchmaker free to concentrate itself on Terra. But acute observation soon showed her that Terra was more admired than sought after. Her haughty and imperious temper was perhaps more on the surface than in the inner nature of the girl, but it operated to frighten off men who would not have been insensible to her charms if these had been softened by a gentler manner. Terra was not the "hit" in society that her aunt had at first expected her to prove. Lady Margreave diagnosed the situation quite correctly, and endeavoured to suggest a remedy. But Terra grew savage with unspent energy, when her aunt tried to keep down her physical activity, and vented her fretful moods on the gentlemen she was set to dance with, or dine beside. She loved as well as obeyed Lady Margreave, so the elder lady had no ground or inclination to be angry with her. The question was simply, whether for her own sake she could be cured of her faults; and when she divined the purpose with which Lady Margreave was trying to cure her, she pleaded for mercy in an agony of protest.

"My own dearest Aunt Mary!" she cried, throwing herself on the ground beside Lady Margreave's chair; the conversation had taken place in Park Street where the Margreaves lived when in town, and the morning after a ball. "Make me a dairymaid at Oatfield, if you like; send me back to poor Papa at that miserable hole where he is stationed; or leave me to live on my own income, my own way, instead of spending it in gloves; but don't set me to mince and simper for the sake of captivating a husband. Oh, Heavens! the notion of marrying a man who could be caught that way. Besides, I don't want to be married, I hate the idea of getting married; I don't like men as such. They make me angry and not tender. I can be friends with them up to a certain point, if they don't want to be tender to me; but then I simply turn furious."

" And show it, my dear Terra, so plainly, that anyone who knows you, can perceive it across two rooms."

" That's wrong of me, as a question of good taste, but justifiable considering the provocation. I love *you*, Aunty, and Victoria Maxwell; and when you get tired of me I shall know it in my nerves, and shall softly and silently vanish away like the baker in " Hunting the Snark." But, till then, let me love you in peace."

She had been sitting on the ground with her arm across Lady Margreave's knees, and now, swinging into a new attitude with the easy grace of a leopard, she leaned her head back on her aunt's lap and held up both hands towards her, clasping them round her neck as she leaned forward to bestow the caress thus invited.

Lady Margreave, who had an eye for female beauty, felt very strongly that Terra was mismanaging her life, though she could hardly rebuke her for not putting herself up to auction in a calculating spirit. She saw that it would be best to wait for events to develope themselves, and so the first season of Terra's association with the Margreave household passed without leading to any results.

It was in the course of the second that she met George Ferrars. She had seen him ride in a steeplechase, and ride the winner. This was at a country meeting during Easter. Ten days afterwards at the Margreave's, in town, he was appointed to take Terra down to dinner. Something happened to his heart-strings during the ceremony—as he afterwards explained to Mrs. Malcolm — and whether it was foolish or whether it was the *coup d'œil* of genius, he knew when he rose at the end of the feast and drew back Terra's chair for her, that he should propose for her at the first opportunity. Terra, for her part, was well disposed to him to begin with. Circumstances had not yet advanced far enough for him to be tender in his manner. Their conversation had been bright and unembarrassed. She started with good first impressions, as she knew at any rate that he was no milk-sop. But they fell into a talk of books and some social movements and the duties of different people in life — drawing-room metaphysics generally—that interested her and made her forgetful of personalities—of her own especially.

"And here, we have never said a word about the Briceborough Cup!" she remarked within a few minutes of the time the ladies were drawn off.

"And it is quite the best that no words should be said about it. My reputation as an *attaché* would be ruined with Lord Maxborough, if he thought I was infected with horsiness, which I am not. I rode to oblige a friend."

"And what has Lord Maxborough got to do with it?"

"He is my chief, my ambassador, the architect, let us trust, of my future fortunes." Then

he added, as the thought crossed his mind
that he would be on firm ground, such as it
was with Miss Fildare from the first, and
surprise her into no concessions which she
might make on the assumption that he was
a greater man in the world than was really
the case. "There are diplomatists, like our
host you know, who are careless of the loaves
and fishes, and there are other diplomatists,
who are constrained to care about them very
much, like me."

Miss Fildare was a hundred leagues from
divining the purpose of this speech, but it
made Ferrars rather more interesting than
before in her sight, as a combatant on the
world's stage. In truth it overshot the mark,
as regards the sense in which she took the
words, for Ferrars, though no heir of large
fortune, had some moderate means of his
own independently of his ornamental profession. Without this he would hardly have
formed the resolution, spoken of already, as
crossing his mind when he drew back Terra
Fildare's chair.

The opportunity for putting this resolution
in practice occurred almost within a week of

their first meeting. Chance had favoured him in furnishing two or three further opportunities of talking with Miss Fildare, but in none of these had he hinted at any deep feelings, or made love in veiled phrases. He had been simple, straightforward, and natural, talking to her about things, places, and people—her own tastes ; and even rather disparaging some of these, for he was too serious in his purpose with her to be insincere, even in trifles.

"I enjoy sport thoroughly," he said, "to put the matter in a paradoxical way, as long as I have a sub-consciousness of the fact that I don't really care about it. If I came to suspect that I did, I think I should turn away from it in disgust. I once heard a friend of mine say amongst a lot of men talking about smoke and drink, and that sort of thing, 'If I found myself with a habit I could not break, I should break myself of it next day.' That puts the whole thing far more neatly and rightly, than if one were to to spread out the idea in a formal logical sentence."

"You're a man, and you always do what

you like, so you never fret for anything. It is only not getting a thing one wants, that makes one want it especially."

"That depends on the thing. About one class of things, what you say is quite true, and the fact that that is so, condemns them really as things not worth wanting. Another class of things—the more you get them the more you want them."

"Money ?"

"No, I don't mean money. In a bad sense what I have just said is true, perhaps, of money ; but it is still truer in regard to having your life fairly well filled with interests that you can respect yourself for being interested in. And it is true, I think, of yet another kind of thing."

The conversation was taking place in Park Street. Ferrars had met the Margreave party at a concert, and had gone home with them by invitation for afternoon tea. Lady Margreave was talking to another visitor in the principal drawing-room. Ferrars and Terra had gone into a smaller room, opening out of this at one corner—a kind of boudoir looking over the Park, to inspect a small picture lately added to its art treasures, and there had remained talking.

"And your other kind of thing, whatever it is, will again be found, I am sure, to be accessible to men only. Women have a poor fate at the best; but as compared with dress and driving about town, I think grouse shooting is a better sort of interest, not to speak of tigers."

"My other kind of thing is not inaccessible to women; and I may as well tell you what it is, Miss Fildare, now, as later."

Terra was standing by the window, Ferrars leaning on the top of a low-seated, tall-backed chair close by, but he did not move from this position, and calmly went on:

"All the other interests of my life have now come to be subordinate to one. Don't be startled at what I am going to say, though I put it very abruptly. I can even explain why I am so abrupt if you listen quietly."

Terra turned round from the window to look full at him, with open eyes, as he spoke across the chair that divided them.

"My supreme purpose in life now, Miss Fildare, has come to be to get you to share it with me. Let us consider why that is so afterwards. First, I want you to know—because I like to be honest and straightforward—what I mean in seeking your society—what I am hoping to persuade you to do in the end."

Miss Fildare was taken too much by surprise to say anything for the moment, beyond a half articulate exclamation of wonder. She leaned back against the embrasure of the window, still looking Ferrars straight in the eyes, but whether with the expression of a hunted animal at bay, or with the exhilaration of a sudden excitement that was not disagreeable, it might have been difficult to determine.

"You are too splendidly honest a creature, Miss Fildare, to tolerate cunning manœuvres designed to win you by degrees. I have loved you altogether, unreservedly, from the first day I met you, and if I did not tell you so, I should be acting a false part every time I came near you. But do not suppose I expect you to come down off your throne, and give yourself to me all at once. Only let me argue the matter with you reasonably, and not be beating about the bush."

" I've always hated the idea of getting married," said Terra, slowly and intensely.

" I don't see why you should hate the idea of being the embodied sunshine of a true man's life; but I divined that feeling in you that you speak of, and I only hope to show you by degrees that it is a mistaken feeling. But first of all I want you to take one resolution, which surely must be a wise one. Do not decide this matter against my wishes hastily. I will be patient on my side. You can see, of course, that I would rather take you in my arms now, than do any other earthly thing——"

" Don't, I tell you, I hate all that——"

" I won't," said Ferrars, still without moving from his first attitude. " That's what I mean —I tell you plainly, I love you utterly and finally, with passion as well as with fixity of purpose. But I do not see that that gives me any rights over you, unless you choose to accept my love."

" I suppose I'm differently made in some way from other women? Most girls, they say, like to be made love to ; but it drives me mad, and it is only because you talk so reasonably in one way, that I can bear it now as I do. Goodness knows it isn't reasonable on your part to want to make love to me. Surely you don't want to marry a girl because you think her handsome, merely, and what is there to recommend me but the outside? I'm a hard, fretful, discontented creature, and I believe I ought to have been a man."

"You don't understand yourself in the least little bit. You might as well show me your hand with a glove on it, and say that is the shape of the glove and not of the hand. Your real inner nature must correspond to the glorious outside you talk about."

" I never said it was glorious."

" No ; that's what I think——"

Lady Margreave came into the smaller room at this juncture to show her visitor the picture. There was nothing odd about the grouping of the young people to suggest that they had been interrupted. Terra left the room while the picture was under examination. Then the visitor went, and then

Ferrars explained the situation to Lady Margreave.

Thus was established the order of things referred to in the letter Ferrars wrote to his sister from the village inn. Terra Fildare was not engaged : that had to be formally recognized by all parties concerned, at intervals, and she would point out with great emphasis that the situation was most unfair and trying to Mr. Ferrars—as he himself would grant in regard to its being a trial ; while pointing out in his turn that his case would not in any way be alleviated if on the ground that it was hard to begin with, it should be made a great deal worse by the destruction of the hopes with which, at all events so far, it was associated. Then, although Terra declared herself simply unable to recognize that she was honestly in love in return, without which, the notion of engaging herself to be married would be unendurable, there were comparatively sunny gleams during the strange courtship to which she found herself subject, when Ferrars' vows of total abstinence in regard to the usual demonstrations of a lover's feeling were a little broken into. There had been, for example, a somewhat greater expansion of sentiment than usual when Ferrars bade her good-bye, before going abroad to his appointment for a few weeks, before the visit to Oatfield, in the course of which he took Kinseyle Court *en route*.

" My darling, that may be," he said, when the parting embrace took place ; " and, my only love, in any case, you are free as air, though I do carry away these sweet recollections of you. Nothing will impair that freedom but your own deliberate choice and spoken word. So do not be afraid that I shall misunderstand a moment's kind impulse when I am going away."

And with this recognition of her irresponsibility, Terra suffered herself to be magnetised for the moment by her lover's enthusiasm, and to be so far responsive as to tremble for a while on the verge of an unconditional surrender. If Ferrars had been less faithful to the promises and principles of his courtship, he might, perhaps, have carried all before him in that critical instant, and later events might have fallen out differently ; but he loyally tore himself away from her without attempting to snatch an advantage from a transitory weakness of hers, and long bore in his recollection the parting look of tenderness that suffused her glowing beauty, and the moisture that glittered in her eyes.

CHAPTER IV.

OATFIELD, though bearing that unpretending name, was a stately edifice of historical interest, with a central painted hall for a dining-room, high enough to be dominated by a broad gallery at one end on a level with the bedroom floor, covered by a vaulted and carven roof and lighted with stained-glass windows. A long picture gallery, with two gigantic fireplaces—themselves elaborate works of sculpture—ran along the front of one side of the house on the ground level, and this, enlarging at the further end into an L-shaped morning-room, and that again opening into the largest conservatory of the establishment, constituted the favourite haunt of the family when no special ceremonial claimed the use of the great drawing-room beyond the dining-hall.

" In the gallery, Sir !" Ferrars was told he would find her ladyship, on his arrival about six. And he passed up the room, hearing voices at the further end, though he neither saw nor was seen till he reached the corner where the L turned. Then he came on a group of people with the remains of tea on a low table in their midst, gathered round the entrance to the conservatory. Lady Margreave was knitting in a low armchair. A dark-haired, bright, beady-eyed, high complexioned girl of middle stature was seated at the tea-table, looking up laughing at Terra Fildare, who was standing just within the conservatory. Terra was dressed in a severe, dark-green braided costume —short for walking—with a small round hat of the same colour and cloth fastened on her wavy mass of red gold hair, and in her right hand she held by the barrels—the butt resting on the pavement —a gun. Within the room was a man in country walking costume—dark brown clothes and lighter brown gaiters; tall, slender, with a close black beard and moustache covering his mouth and chin,

and a long, but not prominent nose that
gave an impassive, rather saturnine, expression to his otherwise undoubtedly handsome face. The two had evidently come
in from the grounds. A footman was
standing near Miss Fildare, having apparently been summoned to take charge of
the gun.

The greetings incidental to Ferrars' arrival,
gave a new turn to the conversation. The
gun was given up to the footman, and taken
away. The young lady herself shook hands
with Ferrars with a certain formality,
ensuing perhaps, from a sense of having
been surprised in the display of that instinct
in her nature with which he was least
sympathetic; and then Lady Margreave
presented him to the two members of the
party with whom he was unacquainted:
Miss Maxwell and Count Garciola.

A meeting with Terra under these conditions was a painful contrast for Ferrars, with
his recollections of their last parting, but he
could only sit down, accept tea, and join
in the talk going on. Terra was taciturn,
and, grandly beautiful though she could not

help being at all times, was in one of her least amiable moods.

"I planned to have you with us yesterday," said Lady Margreave, kindly disposed to make things as pleasant as possible for her guest, whose constraint and annoyance at having no opportunity of greeting Terra more freely, she readily divined: "The Morrisons came over to dine, and we had some nice music in the evening."

"It was very good of you. I should have been here yesterday, but for a mission I had to fulfil for my sister. Life is full of contrarieties. I spent the evening all by myself at a village inn, when I might have been so much better employed."

Miss Maxwell, turning to the Count, detached herself from the dialogue thus set on foot, and picked up the thread of what they had been talking about before Ferrars joined them.

"I think it must have been your story of the bull-fight that made Terra so blood-thirsty this morning, months before any respectably brought up birds are ready for slaughter. If you had us in Spain, Count

Garciola, we should all be wearing stilettoes
and using them on one another in a fortnight,
I believe."

" You ladies are armed with stilettoes by
nature, Miss Maxwell," said the Count, speaking slowly in a deep, melodious voice, with
the least imaginable foreign accent, " and
your eyelids are their sheaths. But you do
not use them most on one another."

" We have got weapons for one another,"
said Terra, " but they are not our eyes.
Some of us find our tongues more deadly."

Ferrars, only half engrossed with answering Lady Margreave's questions about his
adventures *en route*, caught the general
flavour of this badinage with a sense of discomfort.

" That," said the Count, " is no doubt why
you can dispense with the weapons of our
beautiful barbarians in Spain. To carry
the dagger, also, would be indeed super-
fluous."

" I deny that we have any weapons," said
Miss Maxwell. " Leave us our northern
meekness as our only shield. But it is nice
to talk about your southern ferocities. When

is it etiquette for Spanish ladies to stab people?"

"When their lovers are untrue, mademoiselle; but there are ways of keeping lovers true, more certain than the fear of steel—more deadly, as Miss Fildare tells us."

Terra was generally so impatient of sentimental talk, that Ferrars expected her to manifest some kind of contempt for this empty frivolity. But this time she merely answered lightly:

"I would like the steel best. You must send to Madrid and get me a trustworthy poniard."

"What nonsense you children are talking!" said Lady Margreave. "I don't believe Spanish ladies ever use any sharper instrument than a fan. But how did you know where to go, Mr. Ferrars, if your sister merely sent you in search of a young lady without giving you her name or address?"

"She gave me something like the name of the house she belonged to, and I found it out with the help of Burke and the County Directories; and then I, or rather we, for I had a friend with me to share my adventures, came on the young lady, as it happened, in a deserted old house all by herself, in a trance or a fit. It was quite a romantic incident, I assure you."

"What on earth do you mean. Was she a female hermit, or a Lady of Shalott?"

"By no means; there was a governess in waiting and a gamekeeper. The young lady came to of her own accord, and went away."

"But does she live all by herself in the deserted house with the governess and the gamekeeper? You have made friends with a very extraordinary family!"

"And why did you let her go away?" asked lively Miss Maxwell, joining in the talk. "Wasn't she pretty? or wasn't she so young as she had been?"

"She was a charming girl about eighteen or nineteen, I suppose; and yet I came on north next morning," said Ferrars, "and did not try to find out any more about her than just her name and address, which I sent to Mrs. Malcolm. Then my business was over."

"I do not understand the situation in the least," said Lady Margreave. "But diplomatists are nothing if they are not mysterious."

"And when they don't understand situations themselves," Ferrars replied, "then their solemnity gets most impressive. The mystery of the young lady is so far unfathomable. Why she haunts the deserted house in the dusk of the evening; why her governess is frightened to go near the place; why my friend and I find ourselves waiting in an unknown hall for two ladies whom we don't know; why we hear piercing shrieks and rush up to their assistance, and are then told that there is nothing the matter and get no further explanation, I am wholly unable to say."

"Good gracious!" said Miss Maxwell; "this is the first we hear of the piercing shrieks."

"But who shrieked? and why?" asked Lady Margreave.

"I haven't the least conception," said Ferrars, purposely entangling his narrative for the sake of humouring the position. "I think now it must have been the ghost."

"Is there a lunatic asylum at hand, dear Lady Margreave," asked Miss Maxwell, "in case any of us go crazy?"

"Oatfield will be one by the time Mr.

Ferrars has finished his story. But pray tell us more about the ghost. What was he like?"

"I did not see the ghost. I only heard the scream. Then the ladies came away, and I made myself agreeable to the governess, while my friend talked to the young lady, and the house was locked up."

"And the ladies locked out?" said Miss Maxwell. "Then where do they sleep?—on the roads?"

"I don't know; but it is easy to understand that the ghost may prefer to be left alone at night. And, besides, the house does not belong to the ladies at all. The keeper sees them safely home when they have finished screaming."

"I can quite understand that they want a keeper,' said Miss Maxwell. "Does she look dangerous, the Lady of Shalott, or only melancholy?"

"Not melancholy, at any rate—bright and beautiful in quite a remarkable degree."

"We must try and elicit the truth from him by degrees," said Lady Margreave, "when he is off his guard. You must never ask a diplomatist a straightforward question. But meanwhile let us have a little fresh air. Will you come to the garden, Terra, and let us gather some roses?"

Miss Maxwell tripped off to get Lady Margreave a hat. The rest went out into the conservatory, and stood about looking at the plants for a little while, then round the outer door; but when the hat was brought, Terra declared that she had been walking about enough, and would go to her room to be lazy till dinner.

"I will do execution on the roses to-morrow, Aunt Mary," she said, "and make a clean sweep of the old ones all through the house."

Ferrars only had the opportunity, as they moved about the conservatory, of exchanging half a dozen words with her.

"You got my letter from the Hague?"

"Yes; I had no need to answer, as I knew you were coming here. Besides, I had nothing fresh to tell you. I like being in the country, you know, and I've merely been enjoying myself."

"I hope you may do that always, wherever you are."

Lady Margreave and Ferrars went out
into the grounds by themselves after all, as
Terra commanded Miss Maxwell's attendance
on herself, and the Count said he was promised
half an hour with Sir James.

"He's hooked on to the Spanish embassy,
is he not?" said Ferrars.

"Yes; something to do with commercial
treaties. He's a great traveller. He knew
Terra and her father in India. Spent some
time with them, apparently, when they were
at Allahabad."

"He was the hero of the tiger episode in
India then, I suppose?"

"Yes; Terra has a desperate penchant for
excitement of that kind. She is young, and
strong, and full of vitality, and will tone down
in time, I hope; but for the present I do not
think it would be wise to put too heavy a
restraint upon her. That is why I humoured
her whim this afternoon, when she got excited
with the thought of going out with Count
Garciola in search of rabbits. You must not
suppose that she has been making a practice
of that sort of thing."

"I haven't any right to complain in any

case. Whatever she does, lies between her and you."

" It is a trying position for you, Mr. Ferrars, but the way you behave in the matter wins my sympathy, at all events. I hope Terra will learn to be quite responsive in the end, and there is no reason that I can see why she should not. She certainly does not care about anybody else; but perhaps her overabundant vitality prevents her heart from speaking for the moment. At all events, there is nothing petty or unreliable about her. If she does say anything, she is so utterly sincere that you may trust her then altogether."

For the time being, however, Miss Fildare seemed in no mood for discussing any of the questions Ferrars had chiefly at heart. The evening furnished no opportunities for this. They only met again in the drawing-room shortly before dinner, and though Ferrars was directed to take the young lady in, Count Garciola, whose arm had been taken by Lady Margreave, sat on the other side, and the conversation at that end of the table was mixed. During the rest of the evening, after dinner, Terra kept her friend, Miss Maxwell, by her side. There were other guests in the house; some music went on, some whist, and then there was an adjournment to the billiard-room, whence the ladies took their departure to bed finally, while Ferrars was engaged in the uninteresting duties of a four-handed game.

Next morning, Ferrars snatched an opportunity, as people were breaking up from the breakfast-table, to ask Terra to stroll " round the lake "—a small tarn lying within the grounds behind the house, and encircled by a shrubbery. She wavered a little, then agreed; but last of all a certain Mrs. Appleby, an elderly lady of the party who had not heard the arrangement made, was found to be setting out in search of morning air and gentle exercise in the same direction, and went with them, wholly unconscious at first, at any rate, of being in any way *de trop*. The morning would have been fruitless, from Ferrars' point of view, had not they met Lady Margreave at the further side of the lake. She had come round the contrary way with one of her children, and drew off

Mrs. Appleby, making a suggestion at the same time that Terra and Ferrars should go on and give certain directions from her to the housekeeper at Marton Grange. This was an old house half a mile off, belonging to Sir James, and generally let, though for the moment it was untenanted. The walk through a small plantation and across a couple of fields was no great ordeal in itself on a lovely summer morning; still Terra made excuses. Miss Maxwell was waiting to give her a painting lesson—she had merely come out for a turn round the lake, and had promised to be back directly; so the proposed walk was not carried out, though, as they returned to the house, the two elder ladies went on in front, and Terra found herself alone with Ferrars for a short time in the rear. The opportunity was not altogether a favourable one for entering on serious conversation.

"I have a hundred things to say to you," Ferrars began, after a few of the precious moments had been wasted in silence; "but I must wait to say them till you can give me a longer hearing. I am glad to be near you again, but I must hope to find you more at leisure some time to explain to you how glad."

" I hate to be driven," said Miss Fildare. " It was such a glaring thing for Aunt Mary to want to send us off that way to Marton."

" It was meant very kindly to me, and I am grateful for the intention."

Miss Fildare had merely prepared herself for the walk by putting on a broad-brimmed straw hat, and the light-coloured dress of a pliant, woollen fabric that she wore, though loosely made, could not disguise the opulent curves of her magnificent figure. Her firmly moulded features, richly tinted complexion, and large steely-blue eyes, of the kind that have their intensity heightened by a darker shade of colour round the outer rim of the iris, with brows and lashes a shade or two darker than the tawny masses of her hair, drew Ferrars' earnest gaze upon her as they walked along; but she looked up with no answering smile, and her lover's recollection of the all-but-decisive tenderness of her look when they last parted, gave a peculiar poignancy to the disappointment he felt at finding her thus out of reach again and more unconquered than ever.

" Nothing of that kind can be wisely done, at all events," she said in return. " Mr. Ferrars," looking up at him fearlessly and frankly—almost fiercely, " I can see you are of the same mind about me as before. I don't want to be affected about it, but I do want you to leave me alone to choose the time when I will have a serious talk with you during the next few days. It may be stupid of me, but if I feel hunted I can't help turning to bay, as it were. How long are you going to stop here ?"

"That depends! but I will stop until I have had that serious talk with you—or, rather, let me correct that. I am not hunting you ; I am not going to manœuvre to catch you alone ; I will not try to bind you, even by fixing a time for my stay, to give me the serious talk you promise, against your inclination in the end, perhaps. I *am* of the same mind about you as before. Let that be clearly understood ; and understand also, what in your utter freedom from affectation and self-consciousness you may hardly realize always, that I am longing for your companionship— not merely for one talk, but for you altogether—with an intensity that is sometimes almost maddening. But my pride with you—my only pride that is personal to myself in my dealing with you—is that I offer you my great love to take or to leave, and that whatever way you settle the matter, I will hold you in my sight, and in that of the only two people who know of my love for you, entirely in the right and blameless."

"Your behaviour to me is perfect; unless for what was, perhaps, the original mistake of ever noticing me at all. As for me, after all, though the situation may be trying for you, I cannot see that I *am* to blame in any way."

"You are *not*. I do not mean that I will hold you blameless in the sense of screening you from anybody's disapproval: I only mean that I will have the truth in that matter clearly appear and fully acknowledge it myself, if there ever comes a time when there could conceivably be a discussion of the matter."

"I do not know whether that will be or not.

That is what makes me angry with myself. Other girls, I fancy, know, when men propose to them, whether they want to say 'Yes' or 'No.' Perhaps I ought to have said 'No' at once, merely because I was not at once impelled to say 'Yes.'"

"That would neither have been fair nor wise. For you may find it possible to say 'Yes,' Terra, and you may find that beyond such a 'Yes' lies happiness. I do not value myself at any extraordinary rate, and yet—and I have thought over this for hours together, and days—I do not see how you could be unhappy with me, once fairly started with me. I know the reality of my love for you—the singleness of intention in my own character, and its steadfastness in some things."

"I do feel you are honest and true; but——"

They had come back now round the lake to a little rustic bridge leading back on to the lawn before the principal face of the house. The two elder ladies had already crossed this. Terra paused on the bridge and leaned on the balustrade, as though looking at the water, so as not to bring their conversation to an abrupt close by entering the house.

"But what?"

"I do not think what you say quite follows."

"That was not what you had on your tongue to say a moment ago."

"It's quite to the point, at any rate. Suppose it is not in me to be galvanized, even by your feeling for me, into any emotion worth speaking about in return. Supposing I want something in life"—again she paused and hesitated — "something different from love, some other form of excitement—but if I go on talking of vague fancies, you will misunderstand me."

"It might clear up your own mind to talk. It is so important to you that you should understand things and yourself rightly just now."

"Well, I can't go on talking now, at all events; though I feel in a way as if it did me good to be with you. I'm a strange mixture—we all are, I suppose, one way or another."

She put her hand lying on the bridge-rail
over towards him as she spoke. They were
too much in view for him to do more than
take it for a moment.

" It seems as if I were saying good-bye to
you, though we are staying under the same
roof. But you must do, my Queen, about
this glorious gift of yourself, *as* you think
fit—when, and how you think fit."

" Thanks ; you are so loyal ! But I don't
mean that we shall not talk together sometimes, only you must not hunt me."

She looked up with a brighter smile than
she had given him since his arrival the
previous day as she said this ; and then they
went up the lawn and into the house.

CHAPTER V.

"IT CANNOT BE."

If Ferrars may not have been in a position during the next few days to congratulate himself as a lover, he had nothing to find fault with in his treatment at Oatfield as a guest. The party was large enough to keep always in activity; there were plenty of picturesque places in the neighbourhood to visit, and adequate means of locomotion in the stables. Terra generally rode when any excursion took place, and whether she was more perfectly splendid in a habit or in an evening dress, was a question which might have left room for argument on both sides.

The explanation, such as it was, that had passed between herself and Ferrars, had cleared away the embarrassment that had clouded her manner when he first came.

Her behaviour to him was cheerful and friendly, though she made no opportunities for much private conversation. She seemed to distribute herself fairly amongst the three or four gentlemen of the party, who were more or less competing for the lighter favours of her companionship ; and if Ferrars may have been conscious of a keener sense of annoyance when the pursuit of pleasure—the joyous hunt in which they were all engaged—threw her with Count Garciola especially, than when they set her riding beside or strolling apart with anyone else at a picnic, a lover's intuition, rather than any outward evidence of a special feeling on her part, may have inspired his distrust.

" Have you had any private talk with Terra ?" Lady Margreave asked him, when about a week of this sort of life had passed.

They were driving together to the neighbouring station to meet Mrs. Malcolm, who had telegraphed a day or two previously to intimate her wish to come for a few days to Oatfield. She was on terms with Lady Margreave which fully justified her message : " Am wanting a talk with George.

Can you take me in for a few days?" The
reply had been : "My dear, of course." And
when the day of her arrival had come, Lady
Margreave had asked Ferrars to drive with
her to meet the train.

"A dozen words or so," Ferrars replied,
"the first day I came, in the shrubbery ; and,
Lady Margreave, it is coming over me gradually, and now it seems that speaking to you
on the subject has deepened the impression
that I am not destined to have any private
talk with her of the kind you mean at all.
It is all a very simple transaction in its
externals. Terra does not see her way clear
to give me what I want. She can't do that
to oblige me if she is not impelled to do it
for her own sake, and in the absence of such
an impulse there is simply nothing more to
be said. Then Marian's coming down makes
the thing look settled."

"How do you mean ? What has that got
to do with it ?"

"Marian is always drawn to me if I am in
any sort of trouble, and her strange presentiments warn her of such matters in advance.
You know what Marian is in a measure—

and much better than most people. But nobody knows her as I do—nobody else has had the opportunity. All that she calls her inner life is so sacred to her that she never gossips about it; and a great many things happen to her that she never speaks of to anyone, except me, at all events. Perhaps she does not even tell me everything."

"I know she is under some sort of mystic guidance, and has mysterious warning of future events sometimes—or thinks she has. I have never tried to make up my mind what I think about it. She is such an exquisitely lovable woman, so wise and calm and dignified. I could not bear to think she was under delusions of any kind, and yet that sort of thing is so apt to be a delusion."

"That is how I feel, in a way, only more so, and with a difference. It is not a very logical position of mind, because in theory I concur with you that that sort of thing, as you say, is generally a delusion. But all the same, I believe in Marian altogether, more firmly than I believe in anything else in or out of this world. She's totally unlike anyone else I ever met or heard about ; and then, as regards myself, I *know* she knows, somehow, by her own inner feelings, in a general way, whatever I am feeling strongly about, and whenever anything of importance happens to me. It is useless for anybody to tell me, or for me to tell myself, that it is not reasonable. It has occurred too often for me to doubt the fact. I shall ask her as soon as we are alone together whether anything is going to be the matter, and if she says ' Yes,' I shall know that Terra has made up her mind not to have me, just as certainly as if I had had the whole thing over with her."

Mrs. Malcolm, who duly arrived by the expected train, was tall, statuesque, and handsome in a grave and dignified way, with very regular features, that did not break frequently into smiles, with dark brown hair and eyes, a very smooth and rather pale skin, but slighter movements of her face than would have been noticeable with people of more mobile expression would illuminate it with pleasure or sympathy. She kissed Lady Margreave, and then her brother, with tender sincerity, rather than with effusion. Then the ladies got into the carriage. George made arrangements about the luggage, and joined them in a few minutes.

Lady Margreave knew the house from which she had just come. Talk about the people there, and about the party then at Oatfield, occupied them during the drive. Nothing was said between the three about the subject that really preoccupied each the most. When they got back it was still the mid-afternoon. Lady Margreave suggested that Ferrars should take his sister for a turn in the grounds before her things came from the railway; and in this way they all strolled through the principal hall—itself a large and habitable room, furnished with sofas and easy-chairs — and through an archway and passage beyond, leading to the glass door in the other face of the house, which gave on a terrace and the lawn sloping down to the lake. Ferrars was in advance, and he went on to open the door, while the ladies stopped to look at a statue recently added to the adornments of the mansion at the foot of the main staircase.

As Ferrars opened the door and passed out, he saw two persons just crossing the rustic bridge already spoken of, leading from the lower end of the lawn into the shrubbery—Terra Fildare and Count Garciola. They seemed to have been pausing on the bridge, which commanded a favourite view of the lake and grounds. The Count was in the act of turning aside from the balustrade on which he had been leaning, and, bending slightly down to speak to his companion as he went, passed a turn in the path with her, and both of them were concealed from view by the trees. Then Lady Margreave went up the staircase, and Mrs. Malcolm joined her brother.

" Come, dear," said George, as he put his hand through her arm and turned with her to the right along the terrace, " you are as welcome as health to a sick man, though I fear your coming is ominous."

" Ah !" she said, with an expression of pain, " if you feel in that way my impressions may have been an omen."

" My feelings, dear Marian, are nothing to the purpose ; I can only go upon evidences of a more direct kind. But tell me about your impressions."

"Let us turn off the gravel," said Mrs. Malcolm, drawing her brother off the terrace on to the grass, and moving by this change of direction towards the bridge. "We can walk round the lake. I have wanted to be near you, and have been uncertain whether that sprang from a warning that you had need of me, or from my own wish to see you and talk over a matter about which I have need of you ; but I will tell you of that afterwards. First, about yourself and Miss Fildare ; matters are still as they were ?"

"I am not so sure of that. Matters may be worse than they were. Terra, you know, was never bound to me by any promise whatever. It was I who insisted on leaving the question open. I merely asked her for certain things, and begged her to take time to consider her reply."

"You want to shield her from the blame of playing fast and loose with you."

"There is no blame reasonably possible in the case. She so far deferred to my wish as to take time to reply ; but it would be most unfair on my part if I tried to argue that that crippled her freedom of action."

"Have you been talking with her much about here?" Mrs. Malcolm asked as they came upon the little bridge, pausing and looking vaguely about.

"It is about the only place where I have talked with her at all seriously since I have been down here; but that is a week ago nearly."

"Strange. I had a sort of impression about her as we came on to the bridge that— that would not correspond with what you say at all. George, does she love anyone else who is here?"

As the question was asked, the sight of the two figures he had just seen pass up the path they were approaching came with painful distinctness before Ferrars's fancy.

"No one else would imagine it, I believe," he said; "but to me it seems but too possible. But, dear Marian, it will add to whatever I may have to suffer if you are the least unjust to her in thought. Remember, she has the full right to love whom she pleases."

"My poor George, so loyal and true, be at

ease about that. I have a new feeling about Terra Fildare—a sort of sorrowful compassion I can hardly describe. I thought I should come to hate her if she refused you; and yet, now that I realize that she has done this in her heart already, I am only conscious of an immense pity for her. To have your fair choice between good and evil, and to choose evil—that is so sad."

"If her choice turns out evil for her," George began; "but I won't be melodramatic. I can't help loathing the man; but even that feeling may be mean. Why should he not try to win her?"

" Who is he?"

"Count Garciola — a Spaniard. They passed over this bridge together a few minutes ago, when you were talking to Lady Margreave. Let us turn back and go somewhere else."

"They passed here together! Now I understand. Poor Terra!"

"But have you got any painful presentiments about her future, Marian?"

"I know nothing of the man," Mrs. Malcolm replied; "I *see* nothing about him."

Then, after a little hesitation, as they turned away together and walked in another direction, " Perhaps even he is not specially to blame. I may only be guided by the feeling that it is so mad of her to fling away the happiness she might have had."

" Talking with you, Marian," Ferrars said after a while, " is like thinking to myself. I can't leave off thinking about it all, or else I should say, Let us talk of it no more."

Their conversation, however, was disjointed and broken up by pauses. After a while Ferrars asked :

" But tell me, Marian, what was the possible need of me that you had in your mind as another reason for wanting to see me ?"

" It is not urgent for to-day, dear ; but I have need of you, and shall appeal to you as soon as this matter of yours is decided."

" Do you think it is uncertain ?"

" I do not ; but still you must go through some plain explanations, I suppose. Only I think you might exact these without delay."

Some further talk followed about the promise George had given to force no interview on Miss Fildare, and then of many other minor topics, with the major subject ever and anon coming to the surface. When they came back to the house—round to the front again—and returned into the principal hall, they found a number of people gathered there, including Terra and the Count. There was a clatter of voices and laughter going on round the cage of a parrot, who had been giving vent to some general remarks that his admirers had found entertaining. Terra looked even more brilliant than usual. This time she was in a summer shepherdess kind of costume—a pinkish flavour about it, from rose-coloured flowers in the pattern, and pink bows at the throat and elbows, and a looped up skirt. She was altogether bright, sunny and joyous. She had been among the busiest with the parrot, but she left him to greet Mrs. Malcolm as the brother and sister entered. The contrast between the two women—both handsome as they were, both rather tall and commanding in figure—was very striking, and they might have been painted, as they stood together, as symbolical figures of night and morning. Terra's gaiety was quenched a little, however, as she took Mrs. Malcolm's hand—not by any reproachful look she encountered, but by thoughts which arose as they met. From Mrs. Malcolm she glanced at her brother, who said a few commonplace words to her in an ordinary tone.

" And now," said Lady Margreave, " whoever can tear themselves from Polly, will find tea at the end of the gallery. But I shall go upstairs with you, dear, first "—to Mrs. Malcolm—" and see that you are properly provided for."

" Mr. Ferrars," said Terra, turning to him as the group thus dispersed in various directions, " unless you are absolutely perishing for want of that tea, you must first come and see my picture of the old beech-tree. I finished it this morning, and it is on view in Lady Margreave's morning-room. I want your serious and earnest criticism."

The picture of the beech-tree really was in the room, but neither thought of it as they went up a side passage and into the room indicated, which was a little distance off. When they were alone, she spoke :

"I am *so* sorry, Mr. Ferrars, but it can't be."

"I know."

He leaned with his back against the mantelpiece and his arms outstretched on each side along the marble slab. She had come up near to him, with her hands together in sincere and earnest sympathy for him. It would have been almost natural for him to have bent forward to fold her in a farewell embrace, and the impulse to do this half asserted itself in action, but he repressed it and remained still.

"How do you know? What do you mean?"

"I suppose in some strange way my love for you has made me aware of the crisis in your heart that has settled this matter—to my bitter sorrow."

Terra's brow contracted, but more in anxiety than anger, though she began as if to repudiate the idea that she was to blame for having caused this sorrow.

"How could I help what has happened?" Then she checked herself, real regret for the pain she was giving overmastering the strong impulse of her nature to assert herself always in the right. "But I dare say I was to blame for misunderstanding my own feelings. I was a fool not to know if a girl does not feel eager to say 'Yes,' in such a case, she ought to say 'No' at once. I see that now."

"That is as it may be," said Ferrars, quietly enough, though shrinking inwardly at the suggestion embodied in her words that a later experience had taught her how a girl felt when 'Yes' would be the appropriate answer. He moved from the mantel piece and sat down in a chair close by. "It seemed best to wait while there was the faintest chance—and that chance once seemed near——"

"I had intended to say so much to you—to explain things, and to argue that it must be the best for you in the end to marry some one unlike me. And now I feel so sorry. It is like insulting you to say anything, except, that I am so *very* sorry, for your sake, that it cannot be as you wish."

"You could not say anything that would be any good, of course. It is kind of you to feel so keenly about it; but nothing you would say would seem insulting—it would only be quite in vain. I have been mortally wounded, Terra, on that side of my nature, and the rest of my life will be a physical existence without a soul in it. But that is fate. I feel earnestly that it is no fault of yours. That is the only thing that excuses me for speaking in this way, at the risk of provoking regret on your part. However, I would rather, if you will, that you should think of me as true to my ideal love for you, and incurable in a loyal sort of way, whatever happens. It won't amount to anything, of course; but I should like to think that you were absolutely sure, at any time through life, you could call upon me to do anything for you that you might want done; of course, without any notion of having a claim upon you, on that account, for reward or thanks—in a loyal way, I mean. I am talking awkwardly, but never mind. It doesn't matter—nothing matters now, in one way. Do you go abroad?"

"I *must* lead a larger, a more exciting life."

The phrase revealed so much as to the impulses under which she was acting, and as to the little security for her happiness that resided in such a love as that her wilder aspirations had conjured up, that Ferrars vividly remembered, as she spoke, his sister's words about the great compassion Marian had felt for her instead of resentment. A sense that she might be sealing her choice of an evil destiny in giving way to her craving for excitement came upon her lover's heart with the force of a sudden emotion, and almost overcame his self-control. He paused a little while before replying, and she fancied that it was his own pain that was nearly too much to bear.

"Oh, I do hope so earnestly you will find some one to love less of a savage than I am, who will make you happy after all."

"Spare me that wish, my lost love, and remember what I have said."

She moved a step back in the direction of the door. Their conversation was really over, and there was nothing more to be added. But she lingered, hardly knowing how to get away without seeming cruelly abrupt.

"Good-bye," she said, putting out her hand.

"Good-bye," he answered, sadly and gently, getting up from his seat and taking her hand, " and Heaven shield you!" Then he put his other arm round her and kissed her once upon the cheek, she accepting the farewell caress, as it were, with humility. He released her at once, and she went away, slowly closing the door after her.

Ferrars walked to the window, and looked out and noticed a gardener's assistant at a little distance, sweeping up fallen leaves and putting them into a wheelbarrow; and then noticed, as a strange psychological fact, that he had been observing the man as if idly *insouciant*. " I know I shall never get over this," he thought to himself, " and yet I feel more as if I were tired than anything else. I can't face those people at tea. I had better go up to my own room."

He went upstairs with the feeling that something had happened that he would pay attention to presently, but with a numbed sensation of not realizing the truth yet. The physical craving for tobacco, incident on the strain his nerves had gone through, asserted itself, and he filled and lighted a pipe. Then, in a few moments, a wave of painful emotion passing through his heart made him throw it aside ; and it struck him that the small illustration afforded by his behaviour with the pipe would show how all occupations and distractions to which he might turn now in life, would, in the same way, excite impatient disgust directly afterwards.

A knock came at his door in a few minutes, and he called " Come in," knowing well who was there. Nothing but the peculiar relations existing between Mrs. Malcolm and her brother—relations altogether transcending the mere tie of blood, would have justified her in disturbing him just then, or have made her presence endurable. As it was, her coming seemed a matter of course.

"Shall I tell you now what it was I wanted you to do for me, George ?" she asked, without saying a word about the interview that had just taken place, and sitting down on a sofa at right angles to the fireplace— "or would you rather I put it off till to-morrow ?"

"I'm afraid I'll be too stupid to understand, dear," he answered; "or else to-day and to-morrow are all one."

"To-morrow will be worse than to-day, dear. The after-taste of sorrow is always the worse; and she is very attractive. I feel, as I told you, more sorry for her than angry, after all. It is not what I expected to feel; but I may have absorbed some of your feeling into my own nature. We could not feel very differently about this matter, any more than about anything else."

"If you had felt very differently, that would certainly have made the thing worse for me. How wise you are, Marian, on my behalf. I wonder if there is another sister in the world, who in a case like this would have had the sagacity not to abuse Terra? But then it is not sagacity in the calculating sense, with you. It is the perfection of true sympathy."

"I suppose that is so, really. Certainly I am not acting a part in saying what I do."

"I wonder what it was turned her, Marian? She was *mine* when I parted from

her on going back last to the Hague.   Looking back now, I think I might have won a
promise from her then, that might have
guarded her from this."

"If you had," Marian said, "it might
have saved her."

In the completeness of her sympathy, she
was thus capable of even joining him in
blaming himself for the bygone error.

"It is useless to look back upon it now;
and yet, perhaps, if that is really so, there is
one life--mine—perhaps two, wrecked for
want of promptitude and decision at the
right moment, for a single error of judgment;
and that was, after all, a sort of overstrained
delicacy."

They went on for some time with vague
speculation of this kind.   Then, eventually,
Mrs. Malcolm remarked:

"I could never get any guidance as to how
you ought to act with Terra, though I tried
so hard to get a hint.   I once thought I was
going to have a clue, but it never came."

"How do you mean?"

"I talk of this with no one but you,
George; you understand?"

" I know, dear," Ferrars answered gravely. "It is sacred for you, so it is sacred for me, though the thing itself is quite incomprehensible."

" Incomprehensible, but not incredible, I hope, George."

" I believe in you, you know, so absolutely that I believe through you in anything you believe in. I wish my feeling about this were more complete, for both our sakes."

" I suppose that is the nearest you can come to at present. But at all events, you understand that my Guardian Angel is as real to me as any living friend I have—as real to me as you are. In a sort of way, more real ; for sometimes I feel very strongly that to one another in this world we are masked somehow. When we come to know each other, in another, better world, we shall find that we are something different from what we now imagine. People who truly love one another will not be disappointed at the change—quite otherwise, I expect. The change will be some kind of revelation and unfoldment of new knowledge about one another, which will probably be very delightful. But still there will be a change, and for that reason, two loving people cannot know one another thoroughly. Now, it seems to me, as if I already knew my Guardian, as she *is* in actual reality in the higher world. When my turn comes to go there too, I shall find her there as I know her now; only instead of getting mere glimpses of her, I shall be with her altogether—see her face to face without any veil between us—as there is always when I see her now."

"Do you mean by a veil the difficulty of seeing her distinctly?"

"I mean by that what you say, and also an actual visible veil she seems to wear; that, I suppose, is intended to symbolize the difficulty. Perhaps it is impossible for her to make her features quite distinct to me while I am looking at her with the eyes of the flesh, so she shows herself to me with a veil. But it is a veil, you must understand, of the faintest and most diaphanous kind, so that I seem almost to know her face."

"Has she appeared to you often of late?"

"Several times; and always with the same object in view. She wishes me to become acquainted with the girl I asked you to find out for me."

" I thought you said you had been asking about my relations with Terra ?" Ferrars said recurring to the subject nearest his heart.

" I sought to know about that, of course ; but without success."

" What was the clue you thought yourself about to obtain ?"

Mrs. Malcolm paused a little, as if in embarrassment; then she said :

" I do not understand it, George, and you must not misunderstand it. I feel that she could not neglect any promise she made me. She could not speak idly, and yet it would seem as if she had not told me what she wanted to tell. She said, when I besought her for guidance in the matter nearest to you, and therefore nearest to me, that she would give it at the fitting time. And yet, now, the time for advice in the matter has altogether gone by. It bewilders me, for it is my religion, or a part of my religion, that she cannot err."

George was silent. He would not say

anything to wound his sister's most delicate susceptibilities; and yet he felt that in this matter her spirit-guide had mocked her confidence.

"At all events," he said, "I have no misleading advice to complain of; and whatever I have done wrong, has been done through my own folly."

"Don't dwell on that, George, dear," Mrs. Malcolm pleaded. "Sooner or later, I shall come to understand what she meant. It may be that no good advice was possible—that what has taken place had to be accomplished. I do not know—but my Guardian must know—I have told you this simply because I will never keep anything from you; but you will not let it weaken your readiness to help me in following her guidance in the other matter?"

"My dear Marian, whatever you wish me to do, I will do on that account. I do not want any other motive."

"Well, it must be so for the present. I want you to come with me, when I go in search of this girl. I do not know yet why I particularly want that, except that *she* wishes it. That is enough for me. And for you—you say you will do what I wish for my sake."

" It will be easy for me to go anywhere with you, Marian. There is no one else I could bear to be with just now. When are we to go—and where ?"

" I suppose you would be glad to go from here—the sooner the better ?"

" Certainly ; the sooner the better. To-morrow, better than the next day ; to-day, better than to-morrow. But that is impossible, I fear."

" Lady Margreave will understand, and anyone else will accept any explanation she chooses to give. Let it be to-morrow. To-day, of course, is impossible. It is getting to be evening already."

The dinner-party and the evening afterwards proved less trying in fact than in anticipation for the brother and sister. With care for Ferrars' feelings, Miss Fildare effaced herself as much as possible ; was taken in to dinner by an entirely neutral guest, spoke scarcely at all with Count Garciola, who was allotted to Miss Maxwell at table, and monopolised by that young lady as far as possible afterwards.

Ferrars went into the billiard-room after dinner. Lady Margreave, who had been apprised by Mrs. Malcolm of what had occurred, avoided any of the kindly devices she had been hitherto employing to throw Terra and Mr. Ferrars together, and the evening wore away.

By the connivance of their hostess, the brother and sister slipped off quietly the following morning to the station, and no one noticed their departure. Ferrars had no other leave-taking with Terra than that which had already taken place in the morning-room.

CHAPTER VI.

ONE UNION ACCOMPLISHED.

ABOUT a week after Mrs. Malcolm and Ferrars left Oatfield, Edith Kinseyle, as she sat at breakfast with her father and Miss Barkley, received a letter from a country neighbour, Mrs. Graham-Lee. Her acquaintance with this lady was so slight, that she began to make surprised comments as she read the letter.

"Papa, dear, have you, oh! *have you* been paying marked attentions to Mrs. Graham-Lee? Why does she suddenly want to come and see me? Why does she thirst to visit Kinseyle Court? She cannot expect to find a fox there in July. Why does she want to introduce her friends to ' the intellectual lion of the neighbourhood?' Can you really imagine that Mrs. Graham - Lee knows Arabic from Choctaw?"

"And who is Mrs. Graham-Lee, Birdie? and what does she want?"

"Oh, Papa! what dreadful dissimulation. She is coming to Compton Wood to call, and it can't be for me, for she barely knows I exist, and probably thinks of me as aged five. She must have designs upon your heart. It might be a very suitable match, Papa. She belongs to hugely rich people in New York, but is quite settled now in England; Midhamptonshire property — and a blooming widow of forty. But you would have to hunt at least three times a week."

"Is there such a person, Miss Barkley?" asked Mr. Kinseyle. Edith's bright spirits made the sunshine of Compton Wood, and her father always played up willingly to her badinage when they were together. "Or has Edith invented her?"

"Poor Papa! I am afraid you must be far gone. The disguise is too thin. But what's this she says at the end? 'My friend, Mrs. Malcolm, is a stranger to you; but her brother, who is with her and staying with me for a few days, says he has had the honour of a very informal presentation to you already. His name is Ferrars.'"

Miss Edith was caught in her own trap as she read out the conclusion of the note. The name was instantly recognised by both ladies ; and even Mr. Kinseyle, though no close observer, caught the inflection of surprise in Edith's voice.

"So, then," he remarked, though more in the tone of the previous banter than as taking the matter seriously, "Birdie appears to understand everything as soon as a gentleman's name is mentioned. And who is Mr. Ferrars ? I hope he is well connected, and with property in Midhamptonshire."

"My acquaintance with Mr. Ferrars, Papa ?"—Edith began as in exculpation ; but then the humour of the situation caught her fancy, and she finished the sentence in a tone of mock complacency, "is very satisfactory, so far. I really don't know that he has a fault."

"Goodness, Edith !" began Miss Barkley, "why——"

"My dear B., I am *convinced* that you know nothing against Mr. Ferrars either, and you know him much better even than I."

" And who is Mr. Ferrars, Birdie ?　Who does he belong to, and what is he like ?"

" Let us be systematic, Papa.　I can't answer all those questions at once. What is he like ?　Let us deal with that first.　Describe him, B. ; you know him best, as I have said."

" Oh, I don't know.　He is just an ordinary gentlemanly kind of young man."

" Just an ordinary young man !　Why, I assure you, Papa, the only time we were all three together, B. fairly monopolised him. I could not get in a single word.　And I, who was simply *out of it*, can tell you more than that.　Mr. Ferrars is a reasonably tall young man, with an unmistakable flavour of good society.　Thick brown hair, coming forward and rather heavy, don't you know, at the top of the forehead ; short beard and moustache—not a a great straggling bunch, but neat and curly" (making appropriate gestures with her fingers round her own rose-red lips and dimpled, rounded chin), " very bright brown eyes, and a quick impulsive sort of manner. Apt to be carried away by his feelings, I should think, as B. can tell you, no doubt, better than I."

"I will tell the story my way, if you like, Mr. Kinseyle," said Miss Barkley, making a conscientious professional protest against all these insinuations, but aware that submission to Edith's statements, as also to her will in all things, was her first practical rule of behaviour.

"Birdie seems to know all about the matter," said Mr. Kinseyle. "And who is he, besides being—— ?"

"Besides being an ornament to society. Ah, now I can tell no more. We must refer to B."

"But how does Miss Barkley know anything about him. Isn't he some one you have met with the Miltenhams?"

Miss Kinseyle kept up the mystification as long as it afforded her amusement, and then brushed it all lightly away.

"We don't either of us know Mr. Ferrars at all, Papa, dear. That is the whole explanation of the affair. But he and another gentleman with him were visitors to Kinseyle Court one day we were there, and they were presented to us—if by anybody—by Mr. Squires. It was so recently that I happened to remember the name."

Mr. Kinseyle was not given to imagining complications that were not pressed on his attention, and hardly remembered the letter of the morning when the afternoon brought the expected guests. Edith and Miss Barkley watched for their arrival from a little arbour near the house, under two or three tall trees beside the miniature lawn, which commanded a view of the drive. Mrs. Graham-Lee, a prosperous widow of American origin, fond of society and horseflesh, drove up with her guests about four o'clock in a comfortable landau, and then Miss Kinseyle, attended by her maid-of-honour, went to meet them in the drawing-room.

"I have been longing to have Mrs. Malcolm come and stay with me for ever so long," said the voluble widow, "and here she has dropped into my arms at last, like ripe fruit, of her own accord. Didn't know she could come a fortnight ago, but now she's here I want to show her all the charms of the neighbourhood, so of course I have brought her to see *you*, Miss Kinseyle. I wonder would your father come over and bring you to dine with us one evening ? We must talk about that seriously before we part. But, do you know, my dear, it is perfectly appalling how time flies. I doubt if you were born when I was first brought to Midhamptonshire, and here you are looking like a young Queen already. Doesn't she look like a young Queen, Mrs. Malcolm ?" and then, before the other lady had time to reply, she rattled on with other talk about the Miltenhams, in whose care in London she had last seen Edith, and so on.

Edith and Mrs. Malcolm had been gazing at one another, meanwhile, with eager interest on both sides. Edith had previously been thinking more of Mr. Ferrars as the central personage of the afternoon, and less of him on his own account than as a possible link of renewed communication with his friend ; but though on the first entrance of the callers he had been formally presented, as well as Mrs. Malcolm, it was to the lady's face that Edith felt her gaze attracted as if by some powerful influence; and while Mrs. Graham-Lee kept up her stream of chatter, she remained with her eyes fixed on those of her, so far, silent visitor.

"It is a great pleasure to me to meet you," said Mrs. Malcolm at the first opportunity, and the tones of her voice—always sweet, dignified and impressive—imparted a peculiar thrill to Edith's delicately sensitive nerves. A sense of eager curiosity took possession of her, and it was with more earnestness than the occasion seemed to claim that, when Mrs. Malcolm finished her sentence by adding, " I have heard of you before to-day," she asked:

" From whom? Where did you hear of me?"

" I am sure we must have many mutual friends," replied Mrs. Malcolm, " besides my brother, you know," she said with a smile— " if he may be reckoned one."

" You are none the worse for . . . your adventures of the evening when I first had the pleasure of meeting you?" asked Ferrars.

Mrs. Graham-Lee was engaged in telling Miss Barkley some facts connected with her early life in New York, to which she had passed, by a rapid transition, from noticing the peculiar position of independence in which the circumstances of her life had placed Edith, and the other three were together.

"Much the better for them, thank you. By-the-bye, did you think me *quite* insane when you saw me in the moonlight that evening, or only having a fit? But poor Squires was dreadfully disappointed at not seeing either you or your friend again the following day. He thought you were burning with impatience to explore Kinseyle Court from the roof to the cellars, and you never came back at all."

Ferrars answered with lightly-worded apologies. They grouped themselves about the room—Mrs. Malcolm and Edith side by side on a sofa, the others slightly separated; but the room was too small to allow of any confidential talk. Eventually a movement to the garden, suggested by Mrs. Malcolm, and then Mr. Kinseyle's appearance on the scene, afforded an opportunity for a little dispersion. Mrs. Malcolm and Edith moved away, apart from the others.

"I cannot explain to you all at once, Miss Kinseyle, how interesting it is to me to make your acquaintance. But you, I am sure, will understand what it is to be guided in one's action by a higher influence."

The words were not very explicit, but Edith's intuitions were quick. And it was one of her sweetest peculiarities, that though her manner was generally bright and vivacious, it responded instantly to a serious appeal when this touched her inner and more exalted nature. It was with a sweet and earnest gravity, in tune with Mrs. Malcolm's allusion, that she replied :

"I know what it is to *feel* a higher influence. I can see that you will be able to understand me. What a delight! This accounts for the extraordinary effect you have had upon me from the first moment I looked at you. And this, then, is the vindication of Mr. ——, of the prophecy made by your brother's friend."

"My brother's friend? Oh, the gentleman who was with him when he first saw you— Mr. Marston."

"Yes, that was the name. He told me

much that was very interesting in the short conversation I had with him. Do you know him?"

"Poor Mr. Marston? Yes, I know him. I forgot he had been with my brother when you met."

"Why do you call him poor?"

"He has had unusual troubles in life, which have saddened him greatly. He is almost a recluse, but much attached to George."

Miss Kinseyle waited to hear more, but Mrs. Malcolm was not communicative on this topic, and the young lady was shy of pressing for further information. Mrs. Malcolm, on the other hand, questioned her.

"But what was the prophecy you spoke of that Mr. Marston ventured upon?"

"That I should very soon meet people who would understand my inner life and visions, and explain them to me. You seem to have come by appointment with destiny."

"We shall understand one another, and I shall not be the one to enjoy that the least. We have not time to exchange many words yet, but an exchange of sympathy between us may be instantaneous, for we both have some attributes, I suspect, in common."

" Oh, it is so intensely interesting to meet some one who can explain what only bewilders me, though it is so glorious. Do you also see——?"

She hesitated how to finish the sentence, but Mrs. Malcolm accepted it as it stood.

" Yes, I also see; but I am too deeply filled with rapture when that happens to seek any other explanation than my perfect faith supplies."

" But you have had more experience than I. Can I do anything to assist—*her*—to show herself to me again ? Shall you be able to tell me what happens to you ?"

" Yes; I shall be able to tell you as I can tell no one else—not even my brother; for though he sympathizes with me perfectly, and believes in me perfectly, he does not realize what I tell him by the light of his own experience, as you will be able to do."

" Tell me, what is the vision that you see ?"

" An exquisite spiritual being whom I call and think of as my Guardian Angel. I do not mean to assert anything about her by calling her that; I only know that she comes to me from time to time, and especially at difficult crises of my life, and that her influence and guidance are always for good, and that her presence always strengthens and refreshes me."

"It is like the Countess with me."

"The Countess?"

"I think of her as that. There was an ancestress of our family who lived in the room where I have best seen my glorious vision, and where I seem drawn always by a sort of sweet fascination. I don't know, but it always seems to me the spirit of the Countess."

"How does she seem to say about that? Have you made an effort to know?"

"What a revelation it is about you—the mere way you put the question! I know what you mean by 'seems to say.' I could not tell you what her words were, or if there were any, but it has seemed to me that she approved when I have felt sure she was the Countess."

"We shall have so much to recognise in

one another's experience, I can see. And
does the emotion envelope you? You know
what I mean."

"Of course I do; and it is just that. One
seems to be bathed in a kind of ecstasy that
is like no other feeling imaginable. Don't
you remember the effect for days afterwards?"

"I never forget it. I am always longing
for it; but you *feel* it as it were for days
afterwards, before it quite disappears. And
don't you find that it is always right to do as
she tells you?"

"I don't know," replied Edith, "that she
has ever told me to do anything definite, that
I could understand. You know, it is only
quite lately that I have seen her distinctly
when I have been awake. Before that, and
since, I constantly dream about her, and
indeed it seems to me sometimes as if it was
not a dream at all while it is going on; but
then I wake after it is over, as if it had been.
That puzzles me."

"But she does not talk to you in definite
words?"

"I think she does at the time, but it seems

as if I had forgotten afterwards. That annoys me excessively. But when I saw her in the library at Kinseyle Court, there was one thing she said that I remember: 'You will soon know more.' I do not know what it refers to, and most of the time I was simply enraptured at the sight of her, and did not seem as if I had sense to say anything or ask any questions."

"'You will soon know more,'" repeated Mrs. Malcolm reflectively. "Yes; that hinges perfectly on what has been said to me: but I do not know yet exactly how the promise is to be fulfilled, though it must be that I am appointed in some way to aid in its fulfilment."

"Do you mean, then, that what you have been having, relates to me in any way?"

"It relates to you in the most urgent and emphatic way. If I had found you less prepared, I should have hesitated to say that at once; but you are evidently prepared for anything—prepared to understand everything, I mean—that I have to tell. For some time past, all the guidance I have received has been directed to this meeting with you. I have been told to find you out, and communicate with you, and since, as you well understand, my Guardian never gave me your name and address as a living person would—or rather as a person living in the flesh would have done—I have had no little trouble, I assure you, in obeying her injunction."

"Of course; I see. I was the object of your brother's quest when he first came to this neighbourhood?"

"Exactly."

"But what do you think the Spirit, your Guardian, wishes me to do?"

"I have not any idea as yet. My feeling has rather been that I am required to render you some service, but what that is I do not yet understand. The explanation will come now, I have no doubt. So far I have been able to carry out my first orders."

"And your next are to clear my vision by working with me. What! I beg your pardon for putting the idea in that way. It sounds very absurd for me to say what your orders are. I spoke without thinking."

"My dearest child, you spoke under some sort of direction perhaps, without knowing it.   If you did not deliberately frame the sentence in that way, that is all the more likely.   I am more than willing to work with you.   That is it, to begin with, at all events, of course.   For some reason, your senses, beautiful and delicate as they are, are not fully awake.   Your own Guardian cannot direct them freely.   I have been longer under this sort of influence than you have yet, and contact with me may have some magnetic effect upon you; that will clear your vision in the way you say."

They had been walking up and down a long, straight path, running past the back of the house and along the lawn which lay at one side.   They came just at this time within calling distance of the others, who were gathered round the arbour, and some seats out on the grass at the further end; and Mrs. Lee broke into their conversation with an inquiry about the next proceedings contemplated.

"How about our visit to Kinseyle Court, Mrs. Malcolm ?   Would you like to go; and would Miss Kinseyle like to come with us ?"

Miss Kinseyle at once fell back into her

usual bright, every-day manner, declared
herself delighted, and was shortly afterwards
carried off in the landau, Mrs. Graham-Lee
going security for her safe restoration to
Compton Wood. She sat beside Ferrars on
the front seat of the carriage, and for politeness' sake he did his best to talk to her as
they went along, though the scenes he had
gone through at Oatfield had left effects on
him which made even the grace and beauty
of his companion a mere circumstance of the
moment, that failed in any way to thrill his
emotions. It was with a sober, brotherly
courtesy, rather than the spirit of incipient
gallantry which generally warms a man's
behaviour to an interesting girl, that he
asked her now about the evening on which
he had first seen her. Edith was not eager
to go into details, with the double check of
Mrs. Malcolm's and Mrs. Lee's presence to
restrain her, but was answering some of
Ferrars's questions with vague and almost
evasive replies, when Mrs. Lee herself
supplied the antidote to the embarrassment
of her presence by pouring forth an account
of some curious experiences of her own.

These merely had to do with a dream that was verified; but the voluble widow was deeply impressed by the circumstance, and claimed the fullest attention of her companions for all its details. The conversation arising out of this narrative filled up the time the drive lasted.

"I could have wished," Mrs. Malcolm said to Edith, on their arrival at the Court, as they stood aside for a moment together in the hall, "that we had come here by ourselves; but we must hope to do that some other time."

"Perhaps I could just show you the place where I saw her, while the others are looking at the museum?"

A room at the Court which contained an accumulation of Roman stones, together with banners and weapons of the Middle Ages, bore this title, and was supposed to be one of the principal features of interest about the place for visitors.

This arrangement was effected after a while. The museum was on the other side of the hall from the library, and opened into the principal drawing-room of the stately old mansion, whose faded glories of gold and amber brocade greatly caught the fancy of the American lady. She lay back in the corner of an old sofa that commanded a view of a knight in full armour, or, rather, of the full armour without the knight, through the open doors of the museum, and of the rather neglected but still beautiful grounds through the drawing-room windows, and discoursed on the relative merits of American energy and English picturesqueness. Mrs. Malcolm and Edith, who had not followed her into the drawing-room, retreated at this juncture, leaving Ferrars to play listener, and made their way to the library.

"It was just here I have seen her," Edith explained, setting open the door of the Countess's room, and standing before it on the slightly lower level of the library. "It was later than this, however; dusk, and the moon was shining. And she stood, the time I saw her plainly, just here;" and Edith went up the two steps and stood for a little while in the doorway. "Come in here for awhile, Mrs. Malcolm. I used to sit here, mostly, in the window-seat and read; and it was here, indeed, that I first fancied I saw something, and got the idea it was the Countess's spirit.　Poor Miss Barkley was so terrified when I told her!'

" People are always terrified about spiritual appearances, if they have no natural psychic affinities in their nature; and to them it is amazing that we are not."　Then after a little time spent in further talk and in looking about the room, Mrs. Malcolm said: " What do you think?　Might it be possible we should get some sign if we stood together where you last saw her?"

" Let us try!" replied Edith eagerly, and they went back into the library.

Edith pushed a small couch into a convenient position, and they sat down on this side by side.　By an impulse, to which Edith quickly responded, Mrs. Malcolm took one of her hands and held it on her lap, and put her other arm round her.　They sat so undisturbed for some ten minutes, but were not rewarded by any manifestation. Then they heard the cheerful voice of Mrs. Lee approaching, and got up.

" Do you know," Edith said, " I could

imagine some influence comes into me from you? It is very slight, but I can feel a something different in this arm that you have been holding the hand of, from the other."

"I do not think I am magnetic," Mrs. Malcolm answered. "I am in the habit of thinking of myself rather as sensitive to magnetism than productive of it; my brother is for me the magnetic battery at which I refresh myself sometimes. By-the-bye, that is an idea. If he were to mesmerise you here on the scene of your former vision, that might enable you to see."

"I shall be very glad."

"I would rather we had been alone; still, Mrs. Lee will not interfere with us, really; especially if I explain to her."

Mrs. Lee and Ferrars coming in just then interrupted them. After a little interval of general talk as they looked about the library, the couples were rearranged, and Ferrars was left with Edith in the Countess's room.

"You ought to have a web here and a looking-glass. When I told the people I was on my way to see, when I was last here, of the adventure I had had on my way, they spoke of you as the Lady of Shalott, and I have thought of you by that title ever since."

"But I do not in the *least* feel so sentimental as Elaine. I think she made the greatest possible mistake. There was not enough to die for in her case."

"Don't you think love enough to die for ? But in truth," added Ferrars, hurrying on as if to deprecate a direct answer to his question, " I do not see that it is, or can be, for a woman. Perhaps the knights are to blame, and they have gone off frightfully since King Arthur's days. Certainly I cannot imagine a nineteenth century lover worth dying for !"

" And still less a nineteenth century young lady."

" C'est selon."

He uttered the phrase with a half sad, half contemptuous intonation, and not with the implication that might have turned it into a compliment.

Edith said :

" You put it very nicely ; but I am afraid the nineteenth century young lady is too painfully sensible, for the most part, to be very sentimental : or, in other words, she is too selfish and small to be capable of Elaine's beautiful folly. If she is sometimes idealized by her lover, the colour all comes from his own imagination."

" And sometimes she absorbs the colour, it may be, and becomes what her lover has made her in his fancy. Sometimes, of course, she does not—for various reasons."

" That is a pretty idea ; though you put a bitter end to it. It would be the magnetism of love that fructifies in the heart."

" Or fails to ?"

" Or may never be developed. I do not suppose all the knights are magnetic now, any more than in Elaine's time."

" So much the better for them, perhaps ; the ordinary destinies of people in our time do not match well with emotions of romantic intensity."

Mrs. Malcolm and Mrs. Lee here came up into the inner room.

" George," said Mrs. Malcolm, " I want you to see if you can put Miss Kinseyle into a mesmeric sleep. Here, in this old room that she is fond of, the results might be especially interesting."

"If Miss Kinseyle would like me to try, of course," said Ferrars, rather taken by surprise. "But I do not think much of my powers that way, you know."

"You can influence me; and it might be the same with her. Indeed, I feel almost sure it might be."

Mrs. Lee was deeply interested, and arranged herself in a commanding position to observe what took place.

Miss Kinseyle was made comfortable in the large old velvet armchair, and as this was too low in the back for her to rest her head, Mrs. Malcolm sat just beside and partly behind, with her arm extended so that Edith could lean her head against her shoulder. Ferrars held her hands for a little while, laid his own on her forehead, and made passes for some time, but without any startling effect.

"It does not make me feel sleepy," said Miss Kinseyle; "though it makes me feel odd; somehow, I get impressions of a curious kind."

“Can you describe them at all?” Mrs. Malcolm asked after a little pause, during which Edith frowned with the effort to understand something that was perplexing her.

“That is just the difficulty. There is a man and a woman in the matter somehow. I don't *see* them, you know; but the idea of them comes before me, as if of people I have seen some time or other in reality. It seems to me that they are quarrelling. There is such an atmosphere of anger about the whole feeling—as if the woman reproaches the man bitterly, and then turns and rushes away from him.”

“What are they like to look at?”

“The woman or the girl is tall, with red gold hair low on her forehead—massive— altogether like marble.”

The description gave a simultaneous thrill of excitement both to Ferrars and his sister.

“What is the man like?” asked Ferrars.

“Dark—very dark. That's all I feel about him. Black as night. Does it all mean anything to you? I don't understand it in the least.”

"It is very bewildering," Ferrars replied. "It might mean something. At least, I can partly identify the people you speak of. But you do not tell us much about them."

"I have nothing to tell, I am afraid, unless it is two or three words. And I don't know how those came into my head."

" What are they ?"

" As I tell you, it may be the merest nonsense. I don't know why I thought of those words in connection with the woman ; but the words were : 'George, George ! how can you ever forgive me ?'"

Ferrars had desisted from all further mesmeric attempts during the conversation, and sat down now on the edge of the table, saying nothing, but puzzled as well as excited. Mrs. Malcolm looked disturbed and annoyed.

" It is no use to go on at present," she said. " There seems to be some cross influence at work. This was not at all the kind of result I was hoping for."

" Well," Mrs. Lee frankly observed, " there isn't much result of any sort about that. Won't she mesmerise ?"

"It is only with my sister that I am any good at that sort of thing," Ferrars remarked. "We ought to have Sidney Marston here. He really can mesmerise people, I fancy; and he knows all about such matters."

"He seemed to me to know a great deal," Miss Kinseyle promptly added. "It would be very interesting for him to try. But then he is not at hand, unfortunately."

Mrs. Malcolm got up with a little sigh, making no other remark.

"Who's Sidney Marston?" asked Mrs. Lee. "I don't know him, do I?"

"Very likely not," Ferrars answered; "but I don't know anybody better worth knowing. He has all sorts of knowledge, and all sorts of good qualities. I look upon him as my greatest friend. But he's a great recluse."

"What's the matter with him? Has he got a history?" asked Mrs. Lee.

"Well, for one thing," answered Ferrars, "he is very keen upon occult studies of all sorts. Belongs to some queer societies in London that keep themselves desperately secret. I never press him for reasons about anything."

Mrs. Lee now suggested that they had better be going home, and they went out to the carriage.

Ferrars was preoccupied and thoughtful during the drive back to Compton Wood. Edith and Mrs. Malcolm said little to one another, but this little showed them to be both revolving means for another speedy meeting.

"Could Mrs. Lee spare you to spend a long evening with me?" Edith asked. "I want to talk to you about so many things."

"Mrs. Lee," said that lady herself, "is no tyrant, and lets her guests do whatever they like. But if you can, come over to Highton, my dear, with your father or by yourself, at any time. If you let me know half an hour before dinner, so much the better, and if that isn't convenient, come without warning."

Miss Kinseyle expressed appropriate gratitude, but was bent for the moment on having Mrs. Malcolm as her own guest.

"Of course, we shall be delighted if Mr. Ferrars will come too," she added.

Mrs. Lee's good-nature proved equal to the supply of a carriage for the expedition, and it was arranged for the following night but one, some dinner arrangements having been already made at Highton for the following evening, which Mrs. Malcolm was reluctant to throw out.

Edith guaranteed her father's cordial endorsement of any invitations she might give, and, loftily assuring Mrs. Malcolm that it was quite unnecessary for her to refer the matter to him in the first instance, bade her new friends good-bye at the door of her own home with the usual queenly air that so well became her.

CHAPTER VII.

" I SUPPOSE SHE IS BEAUTIFUL."

"SHE's a perfectly charming girl!" Mrs. Lee said as they drove off, "even though she wouldn't mesmerise."

" She would mesmerise fast enough with a better man to manage her, I have no doubt," Ferrars pointed out. " I dare say Marston could put her off in five minutes."

" Why don't you send for him? Where is he?"

" In town, no doubt. He rarely goes away anywhere. But I don't know that he could come. Besides——"

Ferrars looked inquiringly at his sister, without finishing the sentence.

" It is very kind of you, Mrs. Lee," Mrs. Malcolm said. " But—Mr. Marston is a friend of ours, certainly—but it would seem rather abrupt, would it not, if you do not know him?"

"I don't know. I carry my rough American ways with me all about your English society, and I find they answer just as well as at home. The man's a gentleman—isn't he?"

"Most assuredly!"

"And a friend of yours. What more is wanted? Telegraph and tell him we shall be delighted to see him, and that he is wanted at once to mesmerise a charming young lady. That ought to fetch him."

"Perhaps George might succeed on a second attempt," Mrs. Malcolm suggested, rather fencing with the proposal thus forced upon her.

"Oh, stuff and nonsense, my dear! You all say the other man understands the business. Why not have him down and try? Unless 'George' likes trying so much that he won't be turned off."

"George," said that gentleman himself, "is just in the hands of you ladies, to be done with as you think fit; but personally, he thinks he is no good as a mesmerist."

"Well," Mrs. Malcolm was driven to concede, " I will telegraph to Mr. Marston in the morning, if we are all of the same mind then."

The brother and sister had some talk together in private when they got back to the house, before dressing for dinner.

" If you feel so sure about her psychic powers," Ferrars argued, " they cannot have been random words she uttered. Besides, though the few words of description she gave would not have meant much to anybody else, they corresponded so exactly."

" I suppose your mind was filled with Terra's image at the time," Mrs. Malcolm said a little sadly. " She may have caught a clairvoyant impression of her from your thought. As for what was said, that seems to me unintelligible."

" Unless the impression were correct. Unless there has been a quarrel !"

Mrs. Malcolm shook her head.

" That is the sad part of what has occurred. It unsettles your mind ; but I should know if anything had occurred. Lady Margreave has promised to keep me informed of everything that passes. She would be sure to let me know if anything so important as a quarrel had taken place. It is no use worrying you with news from day to day. You will trust my judgment to tell you at once if anything requires to be told, will you not, George?"

" All right, dear; of course."

" There has been no quarrel—nothing in the remotest degree resembling one. It is a mere guess of mine; but the 'atmosphere of anger' she spoke of may have arisen in some way from the contact of the two auras — yours and his — as your thought brought her perceptions into relation with him. I would not dwell upon it."

" There could be no harm," began Ferrars, after a little musing. " But no; never mind. I will leave the thing as you suggest. It is the worst of clairvoyant information, that, wonderful as it often is, one never feels that it is quite trustworthy to act upon."

" Does not that depend upon the kind of action there is to take? Has it not guided me rightly to Miss Kinseyle? Perhaps— you will not misunderstand what I say as implying want of sympathy—perhaps, it is only trustworthy when we have no selfish interests at all involved. Our own desires, however harmless in themselves, may be such a confusing medium. I am sure my Guardian is telling us what is best for Edith. I feel as if she were my sister, and love her as such. We are sisters, I am sure, by our higher natures, in some way."

"She is a very sweet and deeply interesting girl. I should be glad to look upon her as a sister, too, most assuredly."

"I am glad of that, and I should have been still more glad if your influence with her could have been more decisive. It would have been good for you to have been serviceable to her, and I have a strong impression that it is mesmerism she wants to develope her powers. I still think, if you went on trying——"

"It is just a matter, I fear, in which trying is no good if you haven't got it in you."

"It is so embarrassing, bringing poor Sidney Marston on the scene, not to speak of my own wishes."

"But do you think he will come? He will get you out of the difficulty by giving some excuse, you will find."

" I think that, too ; but there is a want of straightforwardness about sending him an invitation, and hoping all the time he will decline it."

" If he does not mind coming, I do not know why we should, under the circumstances."

" There is a want of straightforwardness about it, and Mrs. Lee might not like to have him if she knew.   Poor, dear fellow !"

" Dear old Sidney ! It's awfully hard upon him."

" I suppose he must be judge of the matter for himself.   I will tell him all about how the difficulty has arisen ; though it will seem like suggesting that he should not come, and that is cruel."

Mrs. Malcolm's brow was a little clouded during the evening by the pressure of the situation, but in the morning all anxiety seemed to have been swept away. She made an early opportunity of saying a few words to Ferrars apart.

" I have no doubt any more what to do about Sidney Marston. I asked for help last night, and got it. I am to ask him to come."

So the telegram was sent as Mrs. Lee had desired, and Mrs. Malcolm passed the invitation on with the straightforward simplicity with which it was given.

Miss Kinseyle had not unduly swaggered concerning her authority in the Compton Wood household, when she had invited her new friends to dinner.

" Papa dear," she said, going into her father's study—which was something she graciously forbore from doing during mid working hours—but when she returned from Kinseyle Court it was near their dinner time, and she knew that if Mr. Kinseyle had not left off writing, he ought to be warned to do so. " Papa dear, I simply adore Mrs. Malcolm, and she is going to bless this roof by dining with us the day after to-morrow."

" Goodness, Birdie, but when have we got to have dinner then ?"

" At our usual time, Papa. Do not be afraid I would take a mean advantage of you in that way."

" And does Mrs. Malcolm simply adore you, that she does such an unheard-of thing as dine at half-past five for the sake of your company ?"

"She worships me, Papa dear—but really it is not a thing to joke about. It is not a sudden fancy we have taken to one another, it is a mutual discovery we have made about one another. We are of the same kind. We are natural sisters. She can *see*, also, such things as I see sometimes."

Mr. Kinseyle was never prone to talk much with his daughter on topics of this kind. He was never quite easy about the effect that would be wrought on her mind if she were encouraged to dwell on her abnormal experiences, and he never put an entire faith in their reality, though he dealt with them politely, gently, and with a broad spirit of intelligence, treating the question as to whether Edith might or might not be subject to some poetic kind of hallucination, as a problem that he was not so far in a position to decide either way. He was greatly struck in reality by the statement Edith now made, that she was suddenly in a position to bring up a witness to the truth of her view of the subject; but he was a quiet reflective man, who made no immediate sign of excitement when assailed by a new idea, and he merely now looked into his inkstand with interest, his head slightly on one side, and said, after a little interval, that it was curious ; he would like to talk to Mrs. Malcolm about it.

"You shall have an opportunity the day after to-morrow—owing, you see, to my careful forethought."

When Mrs. Malcolm and her brother came at the appointed time, there had been an interchange of telegrams between Mr. Marston and his friends at Highton. He had declined the invitation to Mrs. Lee's hospitable roof, but had declared himself in readiness to come down, as before, to the inn at Thracebridge for one night, and meet Miss Kinseyle at the old house at any time that might be appointed, when a trial could be made to see if his magnetic powers would be of any service to her. If so, they should be at her disposition.

"But what a singular arrangement," Miss Kinseyle remarked. "Why should he prefer to stop at a horrid little inn, instead of going to comfortable quarters at Highton ?"

"Don't press me, dear, for an explanation of his motives," Mrs. Malcolm urged. "I think he does wisely and rightly, but I cannot explain without breaking confidence I have no right to interfere with. Will you trust me in this matter? SHE has approved. I saw her the night after I was with you last. He is the last man to make mysteries that can be avoided, but he is resolute about not going into general society. I am only surprised that he should have consented to come down at all."

"But how am I to get any good out of Mr. Marston's ministrations, if he can only come down for one evening? That does not seem likely to lead to very much, does it?"

"I have formed a little plan of my own about that," Mrs. Malcolm answered. "If there seems reason to expect good for you from Mr. Marston's influence, I wonder would your father spare you to come to me for a little visit at Richmond. There Mr. Marston could come out to us as often as we wished, and it would be delightful to me to have you with me,"

Edith declared it would be a heavenly arrangement. She was promised, she said, to the Miltenhams for some time in August. They were away from home just then, but were returning to Deerbury Park the following month. If a visit to Mrs. Malcolm could be arranged in the interim, that would be perfect.

"If that would suit your other engagements."

"My engagements of any other sort would be so much cobweb," Mrs. Malcolm replied, "in comparison with serving you, dear, and doing *her* behests."

"It is beautiful to hear you say that. I wish I was as far advanced as you are. For my part—I suppose I have got to live my life like other girls, and I must be more with the Miltenhams in future than I have been. I am eighteen now, you know," Edith added with a grave little sigh, as she contemplated the large responsibility this heavy weight of years brought with it.

"But what do you mean by leading your life?"

"I have thought it all over frequently,"

Edith answered. "I am not an heiress, you see. And Papa's means are small, but even this house and the property belonging to it go ultimately to a cousin we hardly know. The family affairs of the Kinseyles seem to have fallen out very crosswise. All the boys ought to have been girls, and all the girls boys, to have kept the property together. Sooner or later I suppose I shall have to face the common lot, and marry somebody."

"It may be a very dreary lot, if it is accepted merely as a necessity," Mrs. Malcolm returned dreamily, after a little pause.

They were sitting together in the little arbour in the garden after dinner, in the dusk of a still summer evening. During dinner there had been some conversation about Edith's peculiarities between Mr. Kinseyle and Mrs. Malcolm—his questions being of a politely circuitous and careful kind, and her replies veiled by the reserve she always felt in talking to a person without psychic intuitions to meet her own; and beyond feeling that in every way Mrs. Malcolm was evidently a very good and proper friend for his daughter, Mr. Kinseyle had not learned much from what passed. He had joined them for a little while in the garden afterwards, and had then retired to his study, while Miss Barkley had discreetly withdrawn, feeling that her presence was not required. George had strolled off to smoke a cigar by himself, and the two ladies had thus been left together.

"That," Edith said, in answer to Mrs. Malcolm's last reflection, "is just why I have resolved not to shut myself up too much henceforward. If marriage were a thing to take or let alone as one pleased—just as it is with a man—there would be no need to think about it beforehand. But I do not mean to do anything rash. I mean to see plenty of people, and make my choice with great care."

Some listeners might have been disposed to take most notice of the comic side of the young lady's sedate philosophy, grounded as it was on the calm assumption that an infinite range of choice would necessarily await her; but Mrs. Malcolm was never especially attentive to the ludicrous side of things, and only dwelt upon the peculiar hazards that would affect the marriage question with a girl of such abnormal gifts as Edith's.

"But *please*, dear Mrs. Malcolm," the young lady pleaded, "do not think of me as intending to hunt the covers of society for a suitable husband. I only mean that I do not think it would be right or wise for me to go on leading quite as quiet a life in future as I have in the past. Let us talk now of what is *much* more interesting. I shall never give up my spiritual life, whatever happens; you may be sure of that."

Mrs. Malcolm did not press the subject any further, and their talk reverted to the ever-interesting topic of Edith's experiences. This led to some account of her earlier enthusiasm about the white knight, and to a vivacious proposal—a sudden inspiration of hers—that they two should go and watch for him at the gate.

Mrs. Malcolm was inclined to disapprove of the commonplace ghost as an unseemly companion for a budding seeress like Edith, but gave way to the girl's impulsive entreaties.

"It would be such fun," she urged, "for me to tell B.," and she tripped lightly forward to the house calling for Miss Barkley.

That lady appeared at the so-called "schoolroom" window, on the ground-floor, and inquired what was wanted.

"Wouldn't you like to come with us, dear B. We are going for a little walk."

"Why, of course, if you want me," Miss Barkley began.

"We are going to sit at the gate as it gets dark and look out for the white knight. I'm *sure* you'd like to come."

"Oh, goodness, Edith! how can you? Oh, Mrs. Malcolm! pray don't take her to do anything so—so unwholesome and so unnatural."

Edith was doubly delighted at Miss Barkley's easily excited horror, and at the inappropriate charge implied against Mrs. Malcolm, of being the promoter of the enterprise.

"Resistance is in vain, my poor B. Her will is supreme. Nothing but your presence will save me. Unless you come too, the white knight will carry me off, and you will never see me again."

"Oh, Edith! what nonsense you talk. I don't believe Mrs. Malcolm wants to go at all."

"Insist upon my going, on your peril," said Edith to Mrs. Malcolm in a stage aside, and, without waiting for a reply, slipped her arm round the lady's waist and hurried her off towards the side of the house. "Fare thee well, B.," she cried, waving her other hand to the governess; "and if for ever, still for ever fare thee well," her effervescent spirits bubbling over in joyous laughter as they went.

"I was too frivolous for my white knight," she declared when they came back later in the evening, having indeed wandered off, after a little fruitless waiting at the gate, down the briar-scented road, talking seriously again about the subjects that interested them more deeply. They had met Ferrars coming back from his moody stroll, and all three had returned together, Miss Barkley being still possessed with the tremors Edith's unhallowed purpose had awakened in her nervous system.

"It was your fault, B., I am afraid. You

made me laugh, and the knight must have been shocked at my apparent levity. We must try and do something together to propitiate him."

They had tea served in the drawing-room before the guests departed, and Edith sang to them one or two songs, with Ferrars in attendance at the piano, while Mr. Kinseyle and Mrs. Malcolm talked about her on the sofa.

"She has a wonderful flow of spirits," Mrs. Malcolm said.

"A dear child,' her father replied reflectively. "I think I appreciate her in my quiet way. The house is very dull without her, but I am ashamed almost to keep her so much with me. She ought to have pleasure at her age. But she is as good as she is light-hearted, and makes herself contented here."

"She might be in greater danger in a less secluded home. With her gifts and extraordinary charm and her great beauty, the world will be a place for her where she will be too much sought after not to need the most loving watchfulness."

"Is she beautiful, do you think? How

odd I never thought much about that. A child grows up, and one gets so used to her, one hardly thinks of that. Yes; I suppose she is beautiful."

"Certainly she is beautiful; and that wonderful vivacity of manner she has, and her brightness, makes her beauty ten times more effective than it would be if her character were different. Then, with the fresh gaiety of a child, she has the wise thoughtfulness of a grown woman; and yet all that I have said about her is as nothing compared with her psychic gifts—in my eyes, at least."

"I am greatly interested in what you say," Mr. Kinseyle remarked, after a thoughtful pause. "I should greatly like to talk with you more at leisure about her. Your experience and knowledge of the world might be of great service to me in her interest."

She had been singing an "Ave Maria" with the rapt look of a devotee while this conversation had been going on in a low tone; or rather, the conversation had begun while she was preluding, and had been carried on during the earlier part of the song.

" I am greatly flattered," she said at the end, with mock displeasure, " at having secured your attention *at last;* but tears and entreaties would not suffice to make me sing anything more of a serious kind. I'll give you something suited to your frivolous tastes," and with that she dashed into a non-sensical popular ballad of the day, picked up from a comic operetta, and rattled off its absurdities with the keenest enjoyment of the task.

" Papa dear," she said, slipping across to the sofa at its conclusion, and putting her arms round Mrs. Malcolm's neck from be-hind. " Do tell Mrs. Malcolm that by nature I am pensive and intense. Only Miss Barkley has brought me up to sing comic songs occasionally to avert the consequences of over-study."

Mrs. Malcolm had no faculty for badinage.

" Many a true word is spoken in jest," she said, as she pressed one of the small hands put round her. " I can quite understand that you are most your true self when you are most in earnest; delightful though you are at other times also."

" Fly, some one, for pen and ink, to put me that in writing !   But about to-morrow ?" for Mrs. Malcolm rose to go.

It was arranged that Mrs. Malcolm should pick Edith up in the afternoon, on her way to Kinseyle Court, and should afterwards take her back to Highton for dinner.   She could return in the evening, she said, in their own phaeton, which would come and fetch her.   There was no sort of difficulty in the matter, and her father raised no objection.

" What are you doing at the Court again ?" he asked, rather in politeness than from any disposition to interfere with his daughter's liberty.

Mrs. Malcolm looked disturbed.   The purpose of the expedition was difficult to explain, but no one had a better right to have it explained than Mr. Kinseyle.

Edith came to the rescue, however, with an easy grace, though with a sweet little touch of solemnity in her manner.

" I'm going to see if Mrs. Malcolm can help me to see again and understand something I have seen there once before, Papa."

"What do you think it is that she has seen?' Mr. Kinseyle asked of Mrs. Malcolm, with a puzzled air.

"How can we tell? But if she sees what I see, as I believe, she will see what has at any rate been the consolation and noblest inspiration of my life in my own case. Of course, nothing of this kind must be done without your consent; but will you trust me to watch over her for this one afternoon, at any rate? It is so difficult to explain in detail, but at all events, I look upon the trust as a most sacred one."

"I'm sure you will take care of her;" Mr. Kinseyle almost eagerly assured her, in reply to the earnest appeal, "I was not wanting to interfere. I'm sure, indeed, that Edith's own instincts are altogether to be trusted."

He spoke almost apologetically, as if to escape from the responsibility which his own question had threatened to bring upon him, and pressed no further inquiries. The two ladies went upstairs together in search of Mrs. Malcolm's hat and wraps.

"You are wonderfully free to do as you

like, my dear ; almost alarmingly so," Mrs. Malcolm said in the bedroom.

"How funny that it should strike you in that way. I could not conceive any other state of things. I have always done as I like."

"It is an immense responsibility," said Mrs. Malcolm earnestly, picking up her hat off the dressing-table and looking at the reflection of Edith in the glass.

The girl, in sheer sportiveness, was balancing herself on the edge of her fender—a solid, simply-made, low iron rail in front of her fireplace ; and with skirts a little picked up, as she lightly laughed at Mrs. Malcolm's solemn enunciation of this idea, stood on one foot and kept her equilibrum by swaying the other from side to side. She did not notice the intentness with which Mrs. Malcolm gazed into the mirror, but kept her balance for a few seconds, and was then just losing it and all but tilting over against the mantel-piece, when Mrs. Malcolm, with a sort of suppressed cry, turned round, and springing towards her, caught her round the waist.

"Why, what's the matter?" cried Edith, half laughing, half startled.

"Nothing, really, and I knew there was nothing really, but I could not help myself. I imagined you falling."

"But I've fallen off this fender a hundred times.   I can't fall more than four inches."

"I know.   But the picture was too over-powering.   It seemed to me as I looked at you in the glass that the mantelpiece and the wall there had all melted away, and left nothing but horrible rocks and precipices.   It was an allegorical fancy merely, but as you balanced yourself, all your life seemed to hang upon the question whether you would go over to that side or this.   I thought you were going over to the rocks, and I simply couldn't help springing forward to save you."

Edith's fancy was too nearly akin to Mrs. Malcolm's for her to take the explanation otherwise than quite seriously.

"Then was I really falling the wrong way? What a frightful idea.   But I really don't think it was certain which way I was going. It's almost a pity you did not wait to see."

"May I be guarded from ever seeing a bad omen about you."

"At all events, dear, you saved me in time. I did not actually touch the mantel-piece, though I believe I slipped down on the wrong side of the fender!"

"Well, let us make a good omen of it anyhow, and may I be always at hand if you want help, as you go on balancing yourself through life."

CHAPTER VIII.

Mrs. Malcolm and Edith found Marston waiting for them when they arrived the following afternoon at Kinseyle Court. They came alone, for George Ferrars had remained at Highton, and Mrs. Malcolm's companionship released Miss Barkley from her usual attendance on her pupil. Marston met them in the hall, and all three went at once into the library.

"It is very good of you to have come down," Edith said, "for I understand you have come altogether on my account."

Marston was very grave, and almost stiff in manner.

"Thanks," Mrs. Malcolm said to him, almost at the same time as she gave him her hand. "I know it is right for you to have come, for I know I did right to ask

12—2

you. It is a comfort to be sure of that much."

"I feel as though I ought to apologise for seeming boorish in making conditions about coming," he said to Edith, merely bowing an acknowledgment of Mrs. Malcolm's few words, "but,—I never accept invitations." He spoke in an awkward harsh tone, making no excuses for the behaviour which he said must seem boorish; but Edith was too much impressed with the vague mystery which seemed to surround him to have thought of his conditions in that light. Moreover, she was too much interested in meeting him again, having entertained a vivid recollection of their brief conversation on the former occasion, to be critical of minor circumstances. Her feeling of satisfaction at his reappearance overpowered all others, and found expression in the cordiality of her look and manner.

"Then I am all the more obliged and flattered at drawing so confirmed a recluse from his den. With you and Mrs. Malcolm, I feel lifted right out of my own humdrum life into the midst of—I hardly know what—

grand and beautiful ideas that you have got to explain to me. Oh, isn't it delightful, Marian?"—Mrs. Malcolm had taught her by this time to use the more intimate name; "we've got a whole long afternoon before us, we three, with no outsiders to interfere with us. I believe this is going to be a turning-point in my life. Let us all go and sit round the window in the Countess's study and talk. Do you know," she went on a little later, when her wishes had been fulfilled, and addressing Marston, " I realize now that I have been quite anxious all day lest something should have occurred to prevent you from coming ; I am so glad to find our programme is to be carried out."

Marston's rigidity thawed under the influences of her sunny good spirits, and the dawning smile with which he looked at her, in its sweetness and wistfulness, would have shown an acute observer that his stiff manner at first had sprung from discontentment with himself, and not with his companions. If they were not displeased there was nothing left in the situation for him to fret over. As small, slightly-made men often are, he was very neatly dressed, but the merit of his costume had to do with its perfect make and taste, not with any showy characteristics. His bearing was very erect, his dark eyes seemed larger and more luminous than ever, but his voice, when he spoke again, had recovered a softer and more natural tone than that in which his first greetings had been uttered.

"It shall be carried out, if that lies with me, but now let me hear what it is."

"Ah, now I recognise your voice again," Edith said; "I did not, for the moment, at first. But now I remember how you promised me, when we were talking together before, that I should soon be helped to understand my visions, and so forth. Your voice brings back the prophecy, which has been most honestly fulfilled, only you have had to take some part yourself in its fulfilment, after all."

"You know nearly as much about our programme as we do," Mrs. Malcolm put in, "for you know that I want you to put Miss Kinseyle into a mesmeric sleep, in order that she may tell us, if possible, and herself afterwards through us, more about the Spirit she has seen, and what is required of her. Do you think you can mesmerise her?"

Marston turned his head, without immediately answering, to Edith, and fixed his eyes upon her with gentle but earnest interest. She looked back at him with a frank, trustful gaze, and a smile that seemed to meet his answer half way, and then Marston said, in a very low voice:

" I am quite sure of it."

" I am so glad," answered Edith. " I fancied you would be able; but Mr. Ferrars found me an unmanageable subject, and I half feared there might be something wrong."

" And now, having answered your question frankly, let me beg pardon for having spoken as if boastfully of my own powers. But, in anything so serious as real mesmerism, truth must come first, conventional self-deprecia-tion afterwards."

" But please spare us that altogether," said Edith. " Let us have the truth, the whole truth, and nothing but the truth, this afternoon."

" Happily, the truth will not require me

to boast again. The reason why I am so sure of being able to magnetise you is, that I know, at all events, enough of occult laws to comprehend some, at any rate, of your own characteristics. But I will lecture afterwards, if you want me to. That will come best after the demonstration of the fact."

" But I like the lecture. Please go on."

" We have got the afternoon before us, as Edith says," Mrs. Malcolm added. " We can talk quietly for awhile. To be three people together who sympathize with one another on the psychic plane, is to hold quite an occult festival. For my part, I very rarely meet anyone I can talk to about my own inner life, but with you both I can open the sanctuary without seeming to profane it."

" In one sense," Marston answered, "all of us who have an inner sanctuary have it in common with each other. The difficulty is to get free access to it ourselves, whenever we wish. You, and I imagine Miss Kinseyle too, can both retreat into it very easily compared to most of us."

" I am not conscious," said Edith, " of

being able to do anything at all; but I am all attention, and only too eager to learn."

"How shall I explain what I mean?" Marston went on. "In some Indian book, I believe, there is a saying to this effect. At the first blush of the words it sounds irreverent, but that is merely because a truly reverent idea is cast in a paradoxical form: 'Whoso worships God and does not know that he is worshipping himself, to God that man is like the cattle in the fields.' The point of the idea is that, failing to appreciate the highest element in our own natures, which is an emanation from Deity, we remain outside the possibilities of truly human development. We are external to the divine consciousness if we do not realize that there is a fibre vibrating with the divine consciousness within us. Realize that, and you know that in worshipping God, you are at the same time worshipping the highest potentiality in your own nature—preparing it for fuller consciousness—retreating, in fact, into the sanctuary we were talking of just now. That must be an intellectual process only for most of us, but for exceptional people, gifted as

you are, every now and then you see as if
with actual eyesight some manifestation of
your own higher consciousness. I take it—
though I should not venture to dogmatise about
the personality, so to speak, of the visions
you both have seen—that these are only
possible for you because the element of
divine consciousness in you is functioning
more actively than with other people."

"It's very interesting," Edith said, having
paid the deepest attention; "but I don't
feel how it applies to me."

"It is very puzzling at first—the earliest
attainments in occult knowledge are so in-
tangible and so subtle. It is merely a
recognition, in fact, in their proper bearings, of
things you have known all along. When you
reach after a thought in your mind, ponder-
ing how can this or that be so, and then,
when an idea flashes upon you or dawns upon
you, where do you suppose it comes from?"

"I don't know. But everybody has ideas
come up in their minds in that way."

"They do; and all human beings have
some attributes in common. But the ideas
that come up in different minds are of very

varying degrees of dignity, and, not to confuse the matter by dealing with the trumpery ones, let us ask whence do the very elevated ideas come from."

Edith shook her head, merely to indicate that she did not see the answer.

Marston looked at her fixedly. The nature of their conversation was such that he could do this without embarrassment; and she gazed back, absorbed in the subject they were talking of.

"Never mind me," said Marston. He had been sitting in a chair, while the two ladies were in the window-seat of the square projecting window; and now he rose, standing beside Edith, and put one hand on her forehead, visible under a wide-brimmed hat that turned back on the side next to him. "Go on thinking of what we were talking about. When you dive into the recesses of your mind in search of some idea, whence does the idea come? That was the question I was asking."

"Oh, you mean from the higher streak of consciousness you were talking about—the divine element."

"Exactly," said Marston, dropping back into his chair; "which, in your wonderful organism, is so susceptible to an external influence even, that magnetic contact with me for a moment, when I had that idea intensely imprinted on my own mind, was enough to present it to yours, and as that was the idea you were wanting, you recognised it, and instantly seized it."

"How do you mean? Then you were actually able to put that idea into my head?"

"I was able," Marston said, with a grave smile and bow, "because of the peculiarities of the head."

"Why, that's mesmerising me already, before you have begun. Oh, Marian! isn't that wonderful?"

"Yes," Marston himself answered; "it is wonderful: full of just cause for that sort of reverent wonder that is a kind of worship. But keep hold of the idea, please, in all its bearings, and it will throw light on what we were talking of before—the way in which the proper recognition of familiar things may constitute a great advance of knowledge.

The ideas that rise in your mind as you think of a problem—ideas that come into your head—have a source from which they come : a great fountain-head of ideas always abundantly flowing. Along more or less choked and narrow channels all men may draw intellectual sustenance from that fountain ; though in the vanity—which is a sad sort of ignorance really—which makes them repudiate their own best attribute, they will have it generally that they think out or develope such few drops as may trickle from it, for themselves. Now your peculiar gifts—attributes of your organism—enable you to realize some things that other people, at best, can only speculate about, and this among them. If you feel that thoughts may come into your mind from an external source —even though that is only so humble a one as another mind—you will no longer be in doubt as to the possibility that some of your thoughts, at any rate—or subjective impressions, we may call them, if you like—when no companion mind is in the case at all, may come from an external spiritual source, and then, in time, you will do more and be able to discriminate among your thoughts, and comprehend which are so derived and which are relatively commonplace."

" And would that be the way the Countess would talk to me? Is that the way," turning to Mrs. Malcolm, "your Guardian talks to you?"

Marston waited for Mrs. Malcolm to reply, but she only said :

" Let Mr. Marston answer for me. I feel how things are with me ; but he will explain it better."

" I take it that Mrs. Malcolm feels as you, no doubt, will come to feel, that the communication is much more direct. The sifting-out process, the faculty of distinguishing thoughts drawn from the higher regions of our consciousness, from those which arise by simple association of ideas in the lower, is possible for almost any reflective and intelligent people. For you, therefore, that is possible, as I have said ; but for you a great deal more is possible also, because, with your higher consciousness awake and at work, it will show you pictures at least— perhaps very great and beautiful realities belonging to that plane—and then, when the corresponding thoughts flow into your mind, it will be as though such thoughts were plainly spoken to you by the beings of your visions, as, in truth, may be really the case. As I am trying to show, the process will not be only inferred about and worked out intellectually by you, but perceived without an effort."

" It is immensely instructive already. What you have done in putting a thought into my head, by some mysterious influence of your own thought, is wonderful."

"What I have to do is to teach you to appreciate yourself. The simplest way will, perhaps, be the most striking at first. Now, for instance——'

He looked round. On the table in the middle of the room were some books—some of the old family records that Edith had been studying. He went to one of these and opened it at random—in the middle— leaving it lying on the table, and having glanced at the top of the page, he came back to Edith's side, saying :

" The first word at the top of that page is

in my mind. You will be able to read it, letter by letter, through me, as you did the idea we were talking of just now." He put his hand again upon her forehead. "Now, what is the first letter? Say whatever comes first into your mind to say. Don't make an effort."

He remained for a few moments standing silent and motionless, with his eyes shut.

"Good gracious!" said Edith, "it isn't L, is it? I seemed to see an L, bright on a dark background, for a moment."

"Of course, it is L," answered Marston. "That is why you saw it."

"No! How wonderful!"

"Now give us the second letter."

In the same way, after varying intervals of hesitation, but without mentioning any wrong letter, Edith gave three letters successively, "L A U." For the fourth letter she said "K."

"Ah! pardon me. I beg your pardon," said Marston.

"Why; what do you mean?"

"Because it is not a 'K'; it is an 'R.' The two letters are something alike when you try to picture them to yourself, and the awkwardly-formed 'R' in my mind looked to you apparently like a 'K.'"

"But that was my fault, evidently. I don't suppose your 'R' was awkwardly formed at all."

"Miss Kinseyle," said Marston, sitting down again, "I have learned more this afternoon already than I have taught you; and if anything fails with you, at any time, in any such experiment as this, rest assured that you are no more in fault than a perfect instrument is in fault when a musician plays a wrong note. Let me be candid. That was an experiment we have just tried. Perhaps I was wrong to try it; because, if it had failed, it might have impaired my confidence and perhaps, therefore, my usefulness to you in anything you want to do this afternoon. But I divined the perfection of your sensitiveness and could not resist testing it. To have done what you have just done is an absolutely splendid feat. I have known it done before, but it is enormously difficult. To have said that at first would, perhaps, have thrown you off the right attitude of mind; but now the course is clear before us. I have not got to *act* confidence with you — the confidence is established, absolutely and overwhelmingly."

Edith accepted the compliments graciously and pleasantly. They were too obviously sincere to excite any distrust; but she declared herself in need of more explanation.

"And I do not see why the result is not to be accounted for by your own extraordinary power. You must have that, for I feel strange feelings in my head from your hand."

"Well; let it be for the present as you please. I *have* power for the moment, at all events; though it may be you who have given it me."

"But are we not to go on with the word?"

"It is no matter now. You have shown the delicacy of your psychic sense in a manner which is perfectly splendid. It would be waste of effort to go on with that."

"But what was the word, then?" said Edith, going to the table and looking at the open book. "'Laura!' good gracious! there it is—the first word on the page: L, A, U.

I wish I had not been so stupid with the R."

" Stupid !" said Marston ; " you are like a millionnaire complaining that he is poor for not having a hundred a year more than he possesses."

Perhaps Edith was playing with the idea, from her usual inclination towards making fun of things, perhaps she did not dislike the eager declaration of Marston's admiration for her powers ; so she smiled demurely, and declared that Mr. Marston was trying to give her confidence in herself, no doubt.

" At all events, I am getting confidence in your powers, Mr. Marston. What is the next exercise your potent will may be pleased to guide me to ?"

" It is a happy phrase," Marston replied. " My will shall be your guide; for your guide may be your servant all the time. While holding the sacred trust, believe me, it shall always be that, and exercised over your soul at the bidding only of your waking consciousness."

Edith felt the earnestness of the promise without fully understanding it.

" I am sure you will take all possible care of me, and I am not in the least afraid."

Marston bowed. Mrs. Malcolm intervened before more was said, and proposed that they should go on with their project.

" We can darken the rooms a little if there is too much light."

" Yes, that will be better ; but first let me put Miss Kinseyle perfectly at ease. That chair is not comfortable enough. I will bring in the couch from the library."

But Edith declared she loved the old chair, and when this was put back against the angle of the projecting moulding that encircled the window recess, with cushions propped against the wall behind, and a lower chair in front for her feet, she was at last made comfortable enough even to suit Mr. Marston's anxiety on that head.

" I would spare you the trouble," he said to Mrs. Malcolm, as she was closing the shutters, " but I ought to remain quite quiet for the present."

" Of course. I can manage the windows, and there is no hurry. I'll close some of those in the library too."

Edith faced the open door leading into the library as she lay back in her improvised nest of cushions. Marston stood by her side, looking down on her half upturned face. The light of the room was subdued by the closed, but not barred, shutters — not entirely darkened.

"Is it well for you to tell me beforehand what is going to happen?" she asked.

"That will be for you to decide, as soon as you are free to look about you. What I shall be able to do will be to put your physical senses to sleep in such a way as to leave your psychic senses in their natural bright activity. And yet your sleeping lips will tell us what these see, and I am always at hand to draw you back at the least sign that you may make. It is exactly as if you were swimming, with a line round your waist that some one should be holding. We can draw you to shore whenever you look tired or give the order. As for what will happen—that is, what you will see—your own higher consciousness will dictate that, not your humble, though very faithful guide."

"You are so absolutely sure of your power

over me, that you do not even care to assume the masterful tone."

"Yes, in one way; I am so absolutely sure of my power to bring music out of the wonderful instrument in my hands, that there is no need to claim that the music is in my fingers. May I take your hands for a little while?" Edith resigned them to him at once. "Now, as soon as Mrs. Malcolm has settled the shutters and herself in a seat near us, you shall give me the order to put you to sleep, and you will not remember the next minute, as far as this room is concerned."

"How my arms thrill. I thought you would have to make passes with your hands for a long time before I felt anything. You seem to be able to do everything at a word only. Where did you learn it all?"

"Ask them whom you may see presently, if you like."

"I seem to know instinctively, in a vague sort of way. In the school of suffering—is that so?"

"Perhaps."

Mrs. Malcolm came back through the doorway now, and took her seat on a low ottoman a little in front of Edith on the left side, Marston standing beside her on her right.

"Are you comfortable, Marian dear?" Edith inquired.

"Quite, thank you ; and you ?"

"Then I'm off. Good-bye. Put me to sleep," she said to Marston, in a little tone of command, obeying his wish with a subtle sweetness in assuming this, and emphasising the order with a slight pressure of her hand in his.

He brought both of these into one of his own, and drawing the other down over her forehead and eyes, repeated the word, bending close over her as he spoke in a low earnest tone :

"Sleep—sleep—sleep."

Then he left her hands on her lap and made passes over her face for a little while, but she did not move after the words had been spoken, and only rolled her head a little from side to side two or three times on her cushion.

"Tell me what you see ?" Marston said to her, "as soon as you can look about you."

Edith made one or two hardly articulate sounds. Marston moved his fingers quickly about just in front of her mouth, and then in a few moments, though speaking as in the profoundest slumber as far as her physical state was concerned, she said, a little more clearly—

"I'm only just waking up; I don't see anything, except the light. It's too bright to see anything."

" It does not dazzle you, though, does it ?"

" No, it doesn't dazzle."

" What is the scene around you like ?"

" I can't see anything clearly—a sort of plain. There are some rocks in the distance. No ; they are close by. Oh! I am rushing along ; flying somehow."

" Isn't there anyone with you ?"

" I think so—" after a little pause, "but I do not see anybody. Ah——"

" What made you cry out ?"

" We seemed to dash up against a cliff, but it did not do any harm. I hardly felt it. What's this ?"

" Have you stopped anywhere ?"

" Yes, on a kind of grassy ledge, a little

valley up among mountains. It's so pleasant." She smiled, though her eyes remained closed; then, after a few moments of silence, called out sharply, "Take care of that thread."

"Trust me to take care of the thread," said Marston in a confident tone. "Does it seem very thin?"

"Yes; thin, fine, and silvery. I seemed to feel some one pulling at it. It is all right now. Oh!—" in a less contented tone, "where does it lead to?"

"Never mind that now. Look round you. Is there anyone with you in the valley?"

"No, I don't see anyone, but I feel as if some one was with me—some one who loves me. Oh!" in a low voice, "SHE's here. I see her now shining before me. She's a glorious spirit. My Queen!"

"That's right. You have seen her before, have you not?"

"Of course I have; I know her. I have always known her. Now I see the real person. What!—of course I will."

"Will you tell me what she has just said to you?"

For the first time since her trance had

begun Edith did not immediately answer the question, but after a little interval began to murmur half articulate words of affectionate adoration and broken replies to some conversation, which she was carrying on in another state of consciousness. Marston took one of her hands again—he had not touched her before since she had been put to sleep—and laid his other hand on her forehead.

"You must come back to us if you will not answer me."

"Take care of the thread," she said petulantly.

"Tell me what the beautiful Spirit is saying to you."

"She tells me I may come to her altogether soon, if I like. I shall not have to stay long in that horrible body."

"Ask her if we are doing right to mesmerise you in this way, and if that is what she wanted."

"Yes, she meant that; that is why she sent Marian to me. You are to go on every few days, and soon I shall be able to understand all she says better."

"Has she any particular orders for you?"

"What—I'm sure she may, to me, and I will obey her."

"What is that she says?" Marston said very emphatically.

"Don't pull that thread! She says——"

"What does she say?"

"I don't know exactly. She makes me feel heavenly. It does not matter."

"But I must know whether she has any orders for you. Ask her that."

Edith smiled very sweetly, ejaculating "dearest," then "Very well," and then replying at last to Marston's question.

"She has no orders for me, she says, only encouragement. But she will be able to talk more plainly to me later on. When I am more at home with her. At any rate, I'm glad I have not got to stay long down there."

Mrs. Malcolm asked in a low voice, "Has she any message for me?"

Mr. Marston repeated the question.

"Has she any message for Mrs. Malcolm?"

"Who?" said Edith, with a little frown.

"Has she any message for Marian?"

Marston glanced round as if to apologise for the use of the name, but Mrs. Malcolm, quickly comprehending the idea, nodded acquiescence, and Edith accepted the amendment.

"Oh, for Marian! Yes, she says I shall amply reward her for the trouble she has taken, and that SHE is grateful. She smiles, oh, so beautifully. How glorious she is."

"Ask her whether it is not time for you to come back."

"Oh, I couldn't *think* of going back at present."

It had an odd effect for the protest, considering its nature, to take the familiar colouring in this way of Edith's ordinary waking manner, a little emphasis being put on one word in the sentence, and the whole given with her usual assured way of announcing her will and pleasure, when her mind was made up about anything.

"I shall bring you back unless you can tell me that SHE says you may stop longer."

"Don't worry. What? yes; she says I may stay a little longer. Only a little?"— these last words in a pleading tone. "As long as she stays with me I may stop. I am bathed in her sweet influence. It is so perfect. I would never want anything more than this. To be always with her—what perpetual Heaven!" These and a few more disjointed phrases of the same kind were spoken at intervals, and Edith's face, all the while upturned as she lay back against her cushions, beamed with a rapt expression of delight. Presently, however, it clouded. "Oh, she is going away! I will go with her. But I can't; I don't know where she has gone. She has gone somehow—where?"

"Never mind," said Marston, "you will see her again another time. Now you have got to come away yourself, you know; that was what she said."

"But I *don't want* to come away," Edith answered quite crossly. "Can't you take care of the thread!"

"Remember, she told you to come back when she left you. Now she is gone, and you must obey her. So I am going to draw you back, whether you like it or not. Sorry to be rude; but you must come."

"No! no!"

Very gently Marston laid one hand on her head and one on her left side, and speaking tenderly, but firmly, repeated:

" You must come. Come back—slowly, gently now," as Edith moved restlessly in her chair, and made a few sounds as of pettish protest. " That's right ; you are coming back now, aren't you ? Sleep quietly now for a moment." The restlessness died away, and Edith's face sank into repose again, losing the varied expressions that had been chasing one another over her features during her trance.

" That's it !" said Marston. " Beautifully brought back. Now you can wake up as soon as you like." And he waved his hands upward several times in front of her face. " Wake up ! You are all here again, and we are wanting to talk to you. Ah——"

He dropped his hands as Edith suddenly opened her eyes, sat up in her chair, and exclaimed:

" Goodness ! Have I been asleep ? What has been happening ?"

Marston drew back a little from her side and sat down on one of the formal old high-backed chairs that stood near the table. Mrs. Malcolm rose, and came to her in his place, embracing her with affectionate earnestness.

"My dear Edith, you have been in Heaven, and telling us all about it. You have been having a glorious vision."

"I remember, now. Mr. Marston said I should tell him when to put me to sleep, and that I should go off at once. So I did. I don't recollect anything after that. It's perfectly wonderful how he did it in an instant like that."

"But don't you remember anything of your vision? You saw HER, you know—beautifully."

Edith put her hand to her head, and tried to recall something.

"I seem as if I should remember something directly, but I don't know what it is. All I can think of is, that I was somehow told to 'come back.'"

"Ah!" cried Marston. "How stupid of me! It is my fault that you do not remember better."

"You managed her splendidly," Mrs.

Malcolm said. "I am sure you have nothing to reproach yourself with."

"But tell me all about it," said Edith. "I am all in the dark."

"But first, you feel none the worse?"

"I feel delightfully. I am much the better. I don't want to move, for fear of breaking the spell."

"Don't move for the present," Marston said. "In a few minutes you must let me mesmerise you again a little, to restore your physical strength thoroughly. Meanwhile, you can lie quiet, and hear Mrs. Malcolm's report of what you have been saying."

"Do you feel weakened, Mr. Marston?" Mrs. Malcolm asked.

"Weakened? No; certainly not. Tired for the moment, but in five minutes I shall be thoroughly wound up again."

The answer, confident as it was, excited Edith's attention, and there was some little conversation on the subject. Then she wanted to know why she had been so "abnormally stupid" as to have remembered nothing of the vision he had procured for her.

"It is just as I explained before about the R and the K," Marston said. "My fault—-I did not impress upon you to remember."

"I do not object to the theory in the *least*," Edith said. "Whenever I make any mistake, that is always to be regarded in future as somebody else's fault. It is very kind of me—having been so particularly stupid this time—but I will forgive you if you will explain how you could have made even me remember, if you had managed something differently."

Marston did not rise very cheerfully to the airy gaiety of her manner. There was something more wistful than light-hearted in the smile with which he replied to it. In words, he said very simply:

"I ought to have impressed upon you at the time to remember the salient features of your vision. Clairvoyants, who go right out of the body, as you did, frequently remember nothing when they return, unless they are so impressed. What you said about remembering that you had been told to come back, just illustrates the thing. I appealed to you to remember that your guardian spirit had said you were to come back when she went away."

They went on talking over all that had passed, and all the characteristics of the trance, and eventually Edith was put in possession of the whole case, and of all that she had said, except as regards the few words she had spoken indicating the probability of her own early death. Both Mrs. Malcolm and Marston avoided this part of the story, and a look of intelligence passed between them as each saw that the other was avoiding the same thing. They told Edith how cross she had been about her " thread."

"All clairvoyant wanderers from the fleshly prison see this magnetic filament that connects them with the body," Marston explained. " I do not suppose it is really in any danger of breaking, in the mechanical sense of the word ; but the clairvoyant associates an earthly notion with it, and if its attraction draws upon him, will generally get nervous about it."

"And was I very anxious about my thread ?"

"Very snappish, my dear, I assure you, when Mr. Marston would not let you break away from us altogether, and leave us nothing but an empty body; and you showed a reluctance to come back to such low company as our own, after being with spirits in Heaven, in a way that was much more emphatic than complimentary."

"It was disgracefully rude of me, seeing that you put me in Heaven for the time; but like all other bad behaviour of mine, I suppose that is Mr. Marston's fault. Mr. Marston, I am shocked at you when I think that I have been rude."

"This time I am not responsible. That you should prefer Heaven to earth is entirely due to your own characteristics."

"So Mr. Marston managed me splendidly you say, Marian?" Edith remarked, acknowledging the compliment with a pleasant smile only. "How *can* you keep control over me when I am right away in unknown regions, and out of sight altogether? Or am I out of sight indeed? Can you see what I am about all the while, and where I am going?"

"I wish I could. We are not all endowed with the power of consciousness on that plane. The only control I can exercise is a watchfulness over your body, which is still in magnetic relations with your soul all the while. It is drawing upon you continually with its vital attraction, or whatever we like to call it, and when necessary I can somehow augment that vital attraction so that it brings you back in spite of your disinclination to come. That is all the use I am to you. I can drag you back to earth."

"But as I can't get away from earth to begin with without your help, I have not so much to complain of. And if you did not drag me back, should I never come back at all?"

"That I would not venture to say. That there would be danger, even to your life, if you were sent wandering in space under mesmeric influences and not watched over from this side, seems to me probable; but you might return, exhausted as it were, at last, of your own accord even then, and the effect of such an adventure would be very bad for your nervous system certainly. As it is, the use

I am of is to enable you to visit your natural home, where your own affinities carry you, without any risk of physical bad effects afterwards. At all events, I can guarantee you from those."

"I am sure you can. I feel exhilarated, and altogether a superior person to what I was before. But now suppose—since your power over me is so complete—that you send me forth again to seek my fortune, and make me remember this time all I shall see."

Marston demurred to this proposal, however, and Mrs. Malcolm also had a feeling against it. There might be some risks in forcing Miss Kinseyle's capabilities too much at first. She might not be again able so soon to realize the former vision a second time. There were all sorts of psychic risks to be considered. Edith begged to be allowed one more excursion, but with affectionate and respectful resolution both her friends clung to the idea that enough had been done for a first attempt.

"Now, if you will let me mesmerise you a little," Marston said, "to restore your physical strength completely, in case that has been tried in any way, we can conclude the performances."

"Mesmerise me by all means," replied Edith. "I shall go to sleep again under it, and we will see what happens."

Marston took his place again by her side at once, but assured her she would not be able to go to sleep this time, however much she might desire it.

"It is an influence of quite a different kind that is upon you now," he said, as he touched her forehead again, and then began long passes over her, from her head to her waist. "You are not feeling sleepy this time, are you?"

Edith shut her eyes and pretended to be going to sleep, but could not keep her countenance long, and laughed with a mock protest against the tyranny she was subject to.

"Well, then, I submit," she said, as another idea crossed her fancy. "I *will not* go to sleep. This time you shall not put me to sleep. I defy you to do it. I'm sure you can't."

"That's the right attitude of mind at

present," Marston returned, in a tone of perfect satisfaction. " That will prevent you going to sleep, and will keep all the mesmeric influence on the physical plane. Besides, since you *will not* go to sleep, I would not attempt to constrain you for worlds."

" Not even to be goaded or taunted into giving way, Mr. Marston?" said Edith, with an affectation of stiffness. " Do you know, if it was not for one consideration, you would fall under the frightful weight of my displeasure ?"

" And what protects me ?"

Glancing up for a moment with a gravity of expression sweeter, under the circumstances, than any smile could have been, she answered :

" The fact that I trust you altogether—to know best and to do best."

Marston made no immediate reply in words, but looked the thanks that could perhaps only have been weakened by expression. He went on with the mesmeric process for a little while, and then said :

" I think you will be none the worse now.

Perhaps rather stronger and more vigorous than before."

During the conversation that had immediately followed the trance, Mrs. Malcolm had opened the shutters again. They now went back for a time to their former seats in the recess of the window, and fully talked over the achievement of the afternoon in all its bearings. The settlement of a plan of future operations engaged their serious attention. The proceedings of the afternoon had been clearly experimental in their nature. It was impossible on the face of things for Mr. Marston to be constantly coming down from London and meeting the ladies at Kinseyle Court, when no one would be able to understand why, if his business with them was so important, he should not go to one of their houses. Besides, Mrs. Malcolm was at Highton and Edith at Compton Wood.

" There is only one satisfactory plan, and that is for Miss Kinseyle to come and stay with me at Richmond."

" That must be done soon, if it is to be before I go to the Miltenhams," Edith suggested.

" I have nothing to say except that you can command my attendance at Richmond whenever you choose."

" And till we meet again there I fall back into my original helplessness. Can't I do anything by myself, don't you think, Mr. Marston. It is frightfully tantalising to be told one is such a wonderful creature, but to feel all the while the most ordinary sort of clay, incapable of doing anything oneself."

" I do not know enough yet," said Marston, " of the object in view to be able to give any advice. Great spiritual potencies of some sort are clearly interested in you. That you should get used, under mesmeric treatment, to freer intercourse with them, is clearly in the programme, but till they have told us, through you, something more of what is wanted, we can only wait, it seems to me, and go on as we have begun."

" Couldn't I learn something of the knowledge you possess ? Can you tell me any books to read against the time when I shall meet you next ?"

" I might send you some books, if you wish it, but you are exempt really from all need of taking the trouble which we humbler mortals have to take."

" I forbid you to make fun of me, Mr. Marston."

" I'll remember the order if I am ever tempted," said Marston, " but it is not relevant to what I was saying. It is not worth while for me, is it, to prescribe rules for you to follow in order to get blue eyes or golden hair—or to acquire the faculty of clairvoyance?"

" But above all," put in Mrs. Malcolm, "it is not necessary for us to be making any programme for the time between this and our establishment at Richmond. That might be a few days hence, if Miss Kinseyle can arrange to come."

And with the resolution that the plan should be carried out without loss of time they ultimately parted. Marston would not be driven back to Thracebridge. He would not consent to so long a détour for the ladies. They all walked down the avenue together, and the ladies got into their carriage at the gate, Marston setting off on his walk in the opposite direction. He turned to look after them as long as they were in sight. Edith looked back and waved her hand, her face bright with one of her sunniest smiles; and again just before a bend in the road carried them off finally, he saw that she turned and repeated the sign, though the distance was too great to see more.

CHAPTER IX.

THE Richmond plan did not prove quite such plain sailing as in the first instance both Mrs. Malcolm and Edith had supposed it. Mrs. Malcolm came over to Compton Wood the following day to lay her proposals formally before Mr. Kinseyle, but found the usually quiet household already invaded by visitors. Mrs. Miltenham, accompanied by one of her daughters, had driven over from Deerbury Park, on the other side of the county, a two hours' drive, having announced her coming by a letter, which reached Compton Wood by the early post in the morning. An old friend, Lady Margreave, she explained to Mr. Kinseyle and Edith, who lived in Westmoreland, had been asking her to go and stay there. She had arranged to go for a week or ten days, at a date that had now all but arrived ; and Lady Margreave had just written to ask her to bring any of her girls if she was inclined. There was a wedding in prospect, and this might give rise to interesting questions about bridesmaids. It had suddenly occurred to Mrs. Miltenham that she might take Edith as one of her girls. Florence, the daughter then with her, and Edith's principal friend in the Miltenham household, could go, and would be delighted to have Edith go with her. It was a charming house, sure to be full of people, and the visit would be a very pleasant thing for Edith, and an introduction to very desirable friends. Then there would be the wedding afterwards, when she would assuredly be welcome as a bridesmaid, and in any case she had been coming to Deerbury Park in about a fortnight, so it was merely advancing matters a little for her to come at once.

Mrs. Miltenham had taken the trouble to come over about this matter in sheer affection for Edith, and desire to do her a good turn, and the offer was one that could not be treated with any hesitation even. The situation was explained to Mr. Kinseyle and his daughter together, and it never crossed the father's mind that there could be any feeling on Edith's part concerning the proposal beyond gratification and eagerness to go.

"It is hard upon you," Mrs. Miltenham had wound up by saying, "to lose her for a fortnight more than you expected, and a fortnight sooner; but it is such a pleasant opening for her, that I felt sure you would submit to the sacrifice."

"Indeed, I should have been shocked if you could have imagined my selfish desires could stand in Edith's way. I will not pay her so bad a compliment as to say I shall not miss her; but I would not consent to have her stop here on my account. I am ashamed, as it is, to have her with me as much as I do, with your pleasant house always open to her."

"You know you don't keep me with you at all, Papa dear; but I insist on spending some of my time in the paternai halls. I declare, Aunt Emma, Papa, in his boundless affection for me, is always struggling to turn me out of the house. Extremes meet, and if I were perfectly intolerable, he could not be more pressing to have me leave him alone."

"And you do exactly as you choose, my dear, as usual, in all cases, of course," Mrs. Miltenham returned. "But that being the case, perhaps the shortest way will be to ask if you mean to honour Florence and me with your company to Oatfield, as I propose."

Edith was not by any means indifferent to the perversity of fate shown in the overthrow of the Richmond programme, but she was too keen-sighted and self-reliant a person to hesitate under the circumstances. Mrs. Miltenham's offer was one that could not be declined without a much more intelligible reason than any she had to give. If the pressure of her own inclination in the matter could have been quite unfettered by complicated motives, she would probably have obeyed the attraction of her psychic sympathies; but she was unwilling—and vaguely associating the idea of duty with her social engagements, would even have thought it wrong—to rebuff Mrs. Miltenham's desire to bring her forward in the world. She confronted, in imagination, the unfortunate necessity of disappointing Mrs. Malcolm, but saw that what had to be done, had better be done with a good grace. She reviewed the situation in this spirit in the time it took her to cross the room and give Mrs. Miltenham a kiss, and simply said :

" I will forgive you, dear Aunt Emma, for making me out so headstrong, in consideration of your having been so sweet as to come over and arrange this yourself. I will very kindly honour you with my company, and am very grateful to you for wanting it. But it is agonizing to think that I have got three new dresses getting ready with Mme. Clarice, that cannot *possibly* be sent home by telegraph. They were designed for Deerbury Park, and now—but the dilemma is too frightful to be thought of."

" That's one reason why I came over myself, dear. I must understand exactly how you are situated."

Having thus taken a serious and practical turn at once, the conversation was soon afterwards adjourned to Edith's bedroom— where a select committee reviewed the resources of the young lady's wardrobe. Mrs. Miltenham stayed for lunch, the conversation at this meal being occasionally tinged by the preoccupation of the morning.

"You had better telegraph, my dear. I will send on the message for you as we go back through Wexley. It will save a day."

"Ought Edith to telegraph herself?" said Mr. Kinseyle, puzzled. "I did not know Lady Margreave had mentioned her personally."

"My *dear* papa, I am not going to telegraph to Lady Margreave, but to Mme. Clarice! How could we be talking of anyone else at such a moment as this?"

"We have decided that Edith's things must be sent on straight to Westmoreland, and as soon as possible," Mrs. Miltenham explained. "She is very fairly presentable as she is, but she had better order up her reserves."

Mr. Kinseyle apologized for his mistake, and declared that it was a great comfort

Edith had Mrs. Miltenham's judgment to go by in such matters.

Mrs. Miltenham's carriage had been ordered after lunch, and they were all out on the lawn waiting for it, the visitors ready dressed for their departure, when Mrs. Malcolm drove up.

Edith would have preferred to have received her alone, but there was no help for it; and Mr. Kinseyle, having gone up to meet her, brought her round the house to the group in the garden.

Edith received her with warmth, presented her to Mrs. Miltenham, and introduced her cousin Florence; but Mrs. Malcolm's quick perceptions divined something wrong. She asked no questions, and made no reference immediately to the previous evening, but began on commonplace topics with Mr. Kinseyle. The newly-made arrangements were none the less disclosed prematurely.

"Well then, my dear," said Mrs. Miltenham, as her carriage was seen emerging from the stable-yard, "this is Wednesday. We shall see you at Deerbury Park on Friday by the 3.15 train. Come with your

maid to the Milten Wick Station, and I'll
have a carriage to meet you. Somebody's
sure to be with it, to take care of you, and
you'll be quite safe. There, good-bye," kiss
ing her ; " Mr. Kinseyle will see us to the
carriage. Don't both of you come. You'll
be prepared for a long campaign, and I'm
sure you'll enjoy it."

" I'm sure I shall, aunt," going with them
to the edge of the lawn.

She sent lively messages to the other
members of the Miltenham family—especially
recommended that her uncle should be encouraged to bear up cheerfully in the hope of
seeing her on Friday, and waved airy adieus
with both hands as the carriage drove
away.

" And now, dear Marian," coming back to
the lawn, and linking her arm in Mrs.
Malcolm's, " come with me to the arbour,
and I'll tell you all about it."

" It tells itself, dear, unfortunately," said
Mrs. Malcolm. " You are going away."

" I am going away, and our lovely project
is not to be—for the present, at any rate. I
wish things had fallen out differently, but I

have been obliged to consent to accompany
Mrs. Miltenham immediately on a visit. I
would much rather have come to you, but if
you will have me later on—after my Deerbury Park visit, instead of before—that can
still be arranged."

"Certainly, I will make you welcome
then, if you cannot come sooner. It seems
a pity, as things began so well; but we must
trust to the future. It is only your own
welfare I am concerned about, and doing
HER will."

"Shall I ever climb to your heights, I
wonder? But you are independent—you
have no other wishes but your own to
consult. I *must* defer to my seniors, and
live the life marked out for me. But I have
not yet told you exactly how it has happened." And then she went on to give
Mrs. Malcolm all details, and mentioned the
name of the people to whom she was going.

"The Margreaves! You are going to
Lady Margreave's!' cried Mrs. Malcolm,
with more excited surprise in her tone than
she often showed.

"Yes; do you know them?"

"Certainly I know them. I was staying there quite recently. It was almost from there that I came here."

"What a funny coincidence."

"More so than you can realize as yet. It must mean something. But I see—that must be left for your intuitions to discover, my dear."

"What do you mean, Marian? Don't tantalize me in this frightful way. What extraordinary complications are implied in the fact that I should be invited to Lady Margreave's?"

Mrs. Malcolm pondered awhile as she sat by Edith's side in the little arbour, but remained perfectly grave, and would not be beguiled into treating the coincidence as a mere subject of curiosity.

"My dear Edith," she urged earnestly, "I do not love mysteries for their own sake, but one must respect other people's confidences. I can't speak quite frankly as to why I was startled when I heard of your going to Oatfield without betraying other people's secrets. Besides, you will be much more likely to be impressed correctly,

if there is anything for you to do in the
matter, if you are not embarrassed beforehand by knowing too much in the ordinary
way. I was put out and disappointed, I
confess, when I first understood that you
were not coming immediately to Richmond; but now I see it may be ordered
for the best as it is. Will not that satisfy
you ?"

"It has evidently got to satisfy me, or I
must go unsatisfied. But I shall be on
thorns the whole time to know what it is
that is expected of me. And what a nest of
secrets you are, Marian. There is all Mr.
Marston's stock for you to take care of, to
begin with."

"Poor Sidney Marston! I have known
him a long while, and that is how I come to
know his affairs. He has had great trials to
go through—or rather, he has been mixed
up in great trouble for which he has been
in no way responsible, but it has mostly
fallen on him. There is no reason whatever
why this should impair your confidence in
him."

"There; I will not plague you about it

any more. Indeed, I have no petty curiosity about what does not concern me, and I was only playing at teasing you to tell your secrets. You great, calm, strong Marian, I know you would be invulnerable to my teasing, any way. However, I do not believe I shall have any impressions of any sort at Oatfield, with no Mr. Marston at hand to wind up my psychic faculties. You'll see you will be disappointed in me. Do you know on what exalted occupation— worthy of the wonderful creature Mr. Marston made me out—I have been spending the whole morning ? I have been going over my dresses with Mrs. Miltenham, and devising orders for Mme. Clarice—thinking of nothing in heaven or earth but the composition of my costumes."

" It had to be done, I suppose, though I don't mean to deny that I think you were better employed yesterday."

" I am quite sure of it. And, do believe me, Marian, whatever distractions may be forced upon me by circumstances, I shall always look upon my inner life, that can only be shared with you, and any others like you, if there are any, as far the highest and best."

Mrs. Malcolm made no comment beyond gently pressing Edith's hand, which she was holding on her lap. She was too wise and sympathetic to argue that the highest and best might still be apt to come off second-best, treated on those terms, and merely said :

"I shall always feel that way, too, about you, dear, however brilliant the worldly side of your life may be."

They had a long afternoon together, talking over various interests of everyday life, and a good deal of Mrs. Malcolm's own married life, which had been mostly spent in India, amidst a round of social amusements that had deeply wearied her, with a husband who had been kind without being sympathetic— a colourless life, with no specific griefs, but leaving a sense of disappointment behind. The moral of it all, she thought, was that the routine of worldly existence could not but be a disappointment for any person with lofty aspirations. The lesson was of no good at second-hand ; but as she read it for herself, it meant that the true purpose of life lay in a future beyond the conditions of earthly hopes and disappointments, though there was too much to be done for others in this world for any clear-sighted person to sink into a mere forlorn apathy. Towards the latter part of the time their conversation got thus on to a higher level than it traversed at first. Edith's readily kindled enthusiasm for spiritual ideas drew her fully into sympathy with this view, and they talked together for a long while of the beautiful presence they were both familiar with; of the purposes in regard to them that SHE might have in view, and of the mysterious link that must unite them—Edith and Mrs. Malcolm—by reason of their similar relationship to the Spirit of their visions. That the Spirit in both cases was identical, Mrs. Malcolm no longer doubted.

When at last they separated, and Mrs. Malcolm bade Edith good-bye for an indefinite period—for the next day she would have to spend in preparations, and on the Friday she would be going—Edith was more acutely sensible of distress than she had felt at first.

" It is a real misery for me to part with you, Marian, and I am quite out of conceit with my new programme, now that talking with you has made me feel all it costs me. Good-bye. I shall not really be living till I meet you again—only playing a part. May it be sooner than seems possible. I shall do everything I can to bring that about, and I shall write to you *constantly*, and look forward to your letters as my best events."

" I shall be a faithful correspondent, dear, as long as ever you are, you may depend upon it." And then the carriage was suffered to drive away.

CHAPTER X.

MISS KINSEYLE was a good correspondent while at Oatlands, as she had promised to be. She sent Mrs. Malcolm a bright and lively account of her journey and arrival at the Margreave mansion, and one incident of the otherwise uneventful trip had an especial interest for her friend as bearing on her own peculiar gifts.

" I have had a new sort of experience, too, I must tell you," she wrote; "one that seems very stupid and meaningless, but in your superior wisdom you may be able to explain it, and if not you must draw upon the boundless stores of Mr. Marston's occult knowledge. We had to stop at Halford on our way here to get our proper train, and waited in the refreshment-room imbibing tea. As we went up to a table in one corner I saw an old woman sitting there, and was just wondering why Aunt Emma was making for that table, when there were others vacant, when, having looked round the room for a moment, I turned round again to follow Aunt Emma, when, lo and behold !—or rather lo without beholding — my old woman was there no longer. I could not make out in the least how she had got away so suddenly, and asked Aunt Emma what had become of the old woman. She asked what old woman ; and appeared to think I was crazy when I would have it that an old woman had been sitting at the table a moment before. Neither she nor Florence had seen any old woman at all. Then suddenly, a few minutes afterwards, there was my old woman again standing a little behind Aunt Emma's chair, and I somehow felt, though she looked quite life-like, that it was not a flesh and blood old woman at all. I asked Florence, who was sitting beside me, if she saw anybody, and she looked at me as if she was wanting the address of the nearest lunatic asylum. So then I asked Aunt Emma if she knew any-body like so and so—minutely describing the old woman that I was looking at all the while —a dear old soul with a kind, sweet expression, a bit of black velvet across her forehead under white hair, and so on. Aunt Emma fairly started, and said I was exactly describing her old nurse, who only died a year ago. The dear old thing seemed to smile upon her, and then melted away—disappeared somehow, I don't know how. I told them I had just seen her, and, as they know I am not quite canny, they were rather alarmed and uncomfortable about it, and wished I would not go on in that strange way. But I could not feel that the apparition boded any harm, though they were both horrified at me when I said I should like to see her again."

Edith's next letter came a day or two afterwards, when Mrs. Malcolm had already returned to her own house at Richmond, whither she had requested Miss Kinseyle to address her correspondence. She was thoroughly enjoying the pleasant life at Oatfield, where a house-full of people were engaged from morning to night in helping one another to chase the glowing hours, not only with flying feet in the evenings, but by every device known to civilized ingenuity in connection with that kind of hunt.

"It seems ridiculous to say I have not had time to write," she said, "when I have nothing whatever to do but amuse myself; but in truth there are so many people helping me to do that, that I am borne along in a roaring current of gaiety, and have had to display the firmness of a heroine in order to secure a couple of hours to myself to-day before it is time to dress for dinner. And to get this leisure I have had to make Florence read my part for me in the 'Happy Pair,' on pretence that I will not rehearse again with Colonel Danby till he knows his words. For I have to break the news to you that your frivolous friend, whom you destined for training, during this period, of so much more exalted a character, has been found out by her present admirers as possessing genius of a surpassing order in a new and hitherto unsuspected line. I am to eclipse Ellen Terry and Mrs. Kendal, and all the rest of them, as an actress, if I fling myself with sufficient enthusiasm into my new vocation.

And I am to dazzle creation to begin with by appearing in the 'Happy Pair' at some theatricals in preparation here, acting with a certain Colonel Danby now staying here, who has been the discoverer of my undeveloped capacities. Now, I have no intention of going stage-mad, and *know* that all this is nonsense, and that I am merely having some fun for the moment; but to hear Colonel Danby and the rest of them, Count Garciola included, you would think I was the eighth wonder of the world. It makes me wonder whether I am really a delusion and a snare in all my aspects, and I look back upon what Mr. Marston said to me in the Countess's Study, thinking was he too, perhaps, mistaken in me and caught by some shallow characteristics which make me reflect the ideas of the people about me like a looking-glass. Write and tell me, dear Marian, that I am wrong in that supposition, at least; for though you will be sighing over me, I *know*, I *feel*—lost as I am in this ocean of frivolity—I do not want to turn out a delusion and a snare for you. Really—though it seems absurd for me to have the vanity to say it, when I snatch an hour's leisure to do so in the midst of days spent altogether in the most useless and unimproving amusement— however I spend my outer life, I must always be leading an inner life too, that such people as are around me now cannot sympathize with, so I say nothing about it to any of them. It is my inner life which unites me with you, and I would not have that tie broken for all the world.

"However, I must tell you about outer things here, and that is why I mentioned the theatricals. No more of them, except for one thing that I must faithfully report. You know, of course, having been here yourself so lately, that there is a veritable 'Happy Pair' at Oatfield, besides the make-believe pair of which I am part. They are to act in another piece on the eventful evening, in the course of which they have not got to make love to each other by any means, but to fight like cat and dog. They were rehearsing yesterday afternoon before dinner, and some of us were looking on, and I was sitting near them to prompt Terra Fildare if she wanted it. There was somebody else as prompter in general but she had insisted on having me as a prompter all to herself, and I was holding her book and attentively following her great speech, wherein she reviles the wicked gipsy in the most slashing manner, when all of a sudden I got a feeling I have never had before. It seems perfectly ridiculous to say so, but I can only describe it as a feeling of *horror!* There was nothing whatever to cause it. The room was half full of people; it was daylight still; we were all in the midst of laughing and talking, and above all I saw nothing—nothing, I mean, of *our sort* that other people do not see—to explain the feeling. Then again, you know, it does not horrify or frighten me in the least when I really do see apparitions. Well, I felt my flesh creep all over, and a trembling set in just as I can imagine I might feel if I were suddenly to see a murder committed; and *then*, for the first time, it flashed upon me what I had not understood before, about Terra Fildare and Count Garciola.

"Do you remember when Mr. Ferrars tried to mesmerise me at Kinseyle Court, and I told you something about a man and a woman and an atmosphere of anger or quarrelling around them ? I had been vaguely puzzled about them from the first time we met, with a sort of sense of having seen them before ; and though I could not identify it, I came to the conclusion that I might have seen them, without being introduced, some- where in London last year, when I was with the Miltenhams.   But all at once it came over me like a flash yesterday that where I saw them before was in that queer sort of half-and-half vision at Kinseyle Court.   I tell you, dear Marian, I *recognised* them. Don't tell me I am dreaming—but I know you will not do that.   You will understand me, and be able to give some wise explanation of my strange feeling.   It did not altogether pass off for a long time.   What does it mean ? If I foresaw, in some clairvoyant way I do not understand, their theatrical quarrel, it makes out my impression to have been very ridiculous, because there is no real quarrel in that at all.   They are devoted to one another really, and though Terra Fildare is reserved and haughty about it before people, I know she unbends tremendously at other times to make up. And why should I get so absurdly frightened and overcome about a ridiculous make-believe emotion in a drawing-room play ? Explain, explain, my sorceress and oracle ! Rede me the riddle."

Mrs. Malcolm was deeply perplexed by this slight and shadowy incident. Starting with the assumption that there was some especial significance in the circumstances that had taken Edith into the presence of Terra and her new lover just at this juncture, she had carefully refrained from saying a word to Edith which might have set her imagination to work in regard to those two persons. But she (Mrs. Malcolm) had been on the look-out for some sign of an occult character through the clairvoyante which might give the clue to the mystery. Here, quite spontaneously, a sign, such as it was, seemed to have come ; but what was to be made of it ?

"I am utterly helpless," she wrote, "in regard to your strange experience about Miss Fildare and Count Garciola, but I am very far from treating it as unimportant or meaningless. It is bitterly tantalizing to be so built round by circumstances of the world and society that our best nature is only to be developed at stray moments that can be caught at in passing, when the serious business of worldliness, which is of such little moment in the long run, may happen to allow. If you could only be put into a proper trance, and *asked* what is the meaning of the impression you had, we should know all about it, and if there is any important warning lurking in the sign sent to you, we might all be guided by it. I would do anything to have you with me for half an hour only, with Mr. Marston to put you off—since he has the right influence which suits you—but I can only fret against the fate that does not permit this. Are you surprised that I take the thing so seriously? If people of the world would only realize sometimes how frivolous are the things they treat so serious, and how serious some of the trifles they put aside with contempt! Perhaps Terra Fildare is in face of some danger, of which the threatrical quarrel is a mere symbol, and we are half warned of it, without, unless we can learn more, being able to give her any warning of the smallest value. Dear Edith, don't think of me as sighing over your worldliness in a gloomy and Puritanical way, because you are enjoying your life and your youth, and the very natural admiration of the people round you ; but all I entreat is, do not forget that you have faculties and senses that may render important the least of your fancies and impressions as they cross the current of your amusements, which may obscure but cannot quench your higher intuitions.   If you notice any other strange and apparently causeless feelings about Miss Fildare or her betrothed, do not treat the least of them as insignificant. Tell me about them, I implore you.   More may hang on this than you imagine, for I may tell you now that, owing to my own feelings, I had been *expecting* you to have some abnormal impressions of that kind, though I could not in the least foresee what they would be."

Edith was set on the *qui vive* for impressions concerning the betrothed couple by the receipt of this letter ; but the days went on without bringing her fresh warning. She tried to make friends with Terra Fildare ; but the two girls, though unconscious of any reasons why they should not coalesce, did not, as a matter of fact, grow closely sympathetic. And they were kept apart, to some extent, by circumstances, as Terra was pre-occupied by her love affairs, while Edith, being game on the wing, so to speak —not yet brought down by any man's gun— was more pursued by general admiration. Two young men staying in the house—a captain of Hussars and a political private secretary — both engaged with fishing as the serious occupation of life, made fierce love to her in their leisure hours, and the Colonel Danby to whom reference had been made in her letter coached her in the histrionic art. The Colonel was a handsome widower, between forty and fifty, rich and well connected, tall, slightly built, a mirror of fashion as regards his dress, with bright grey eyes, a moustache dappled with grey, dark brown hair that only showed the effects of time by a gradual disappearance from the crown of the head, while above his temples it still waved with moderate luxuriance. With a faintly lackadaisical manner, he was, nevertheless, a man of taste and intelligence

and always expressed himself with an easy
finish of language that corresponded to his
somewhat dandified toilet.

Coaching a young lady, recommended by
good looks and a bright gaiety of disposition,
in a sentimental comedietta, is a seductive
occupation.

Colonel Danby declared that the natural
gifts Miss Kinseyle possessed were so undeniable, that it really was worth while to
take trouble—and he was an acknowledged
professor on the amateur stage.

"You only want drilling in details," he
explained, after they had gone through the
most critical scene towards the end of the
piece twice one afternoon, and he was suggesting a third repetition of certain "business." "No two young actresses can be
trained alike. Some, if they are badly off
for brains or hearts, must be taught to
simulate the emotions they ought to feel
as they act. They are the pupils who
always tell you they will do what you want
all right on the night—and they never
do !"

" But they get off so much drilling in that

way—clever girls! From this moment I resolve to trust to the inspirations of the night."

"Do, by all means. That is a safe course for you, because the brains and the heart will give you the right inspiration. But you have fallen headlong into my snare. I am never attempting to teach you how to display emotion. I leave that to your own imagination. I am teaching you the mechanical business, the drudgery of your art. That's a matter of knowledge, and not of inspiration, and so I can help you. Feeling may give you the right expression when you say your best bits; but for want of knowledge you may turn your back to the audience when the features pass through their most delicate crises."

"And for the penalty of having fallen into your snare am I to lacerate my heart over your cruelty a third time this afternoon?"

"Never mind giving rein to the imagination now. I do not *ask* you to wear out your feeling for the part, but to get into the habit of standing in the right places at the right time, making the right gestures, and so on. Then on the night your performance is ready to be illuminated by the poetry of feeling turned fully on. In the dramatic art as in all others there is a *technique* which has nothing to do with its poetry, but without which the poetry will never be transmitted to the spectator."

" Once more into the breach, then; once more let us toil at our pleasure."

" And if one young lady, through this little experience, should realize that to get pleasure worth having one must toil, the afternoon will not certainly be thrown away."

" Are we all so frivolous as that would imply ?"

" Not taught in the same school that men go through, the school of life, that shows exertion and enjoyment everywhere hand-in-hand. The boy learns the lesson at football and cricket, the man in the hunting-field and in his profession, or in political life, perhaps ; and every man worth having acts on the principle by instinct. A girl floats into the world without always realizing the secret that unlocks its best treasure."

" But if they are lazy, and other people are good-natured, it may be so nice for them to be saved all trouble."

" Saved all trouble, all hard exertion, all rough contests beyond their strength—yes, by all means. That is according to the fitness of things. But though the men who shield them and take trouble for them may enjoy their task most keenly, the women themselves, who take no trouble, will enjoy life least. The rough and violent trouble of this life is for men to take ; but, believe me, women in their way may be the counterparts of those keen sportsmen of the sterner sex, who get the best out of life in all directions."

" I never supposed you were so desperately energetic a person."

" Because I am cool in my movements, and behave quietly and dress like a gentleman. One may be a keen sportsman in costume even ; and if a man wants to make himself as presentable as he can he must take pains, though the pains taken may not be paraded. Let us come back to our play. The enjoyment other people will take in seeing you act will be somewhat greater if you act well than if you act badly. But the difference in the enjoyment *you* will derive from it, according to whether you take trouble beforehand and act well, or let everything slide and act as badly as your natural gifts will allow you, will be immense."

"Your wisdom is overwhelming, but I am so sure to enjoy myself *when the play is over*, that I can't feel terrified by your warning. Nevertheless, you have vanquished me in argument, and I am your prisoner. Command me, and I recommence my sobs; standing with the right foot foremost and the handkerchief in both hands, is it not——"

"What?" cried Terra Fildare, coming into the drawing-room where the rehearsals were going on, "you poor, dear, over-driven slave, are you still in the hands of the overseer? I thought you were liberated an hour ago."

"To quote my maid, I am 'that stupid' that I have got to go over the last scene again. I forgot to tell you that, Colonel Danby. It was such lovely criticism—it was so straightforward. 'Is it much trouble learning to act, miss?' my maid asked me last night. 'Frightful trouble for me, Simcox,' I told her. 'That's the worst of learning anything, miss,' she answered; 'and if one is that stupid about it, I don't think it's worth while.'"

"For a mimic with your talents, Miss Kinseyle, I should say Simcox must be a perfect treasure."

"But I want you to try that duet with me," said Terra. "Is there any distant future when you will get out of Colonel Danby's clutches?"

"Certainly not," said the gentleman named, "if Colonel Danby is permitted to decide. The 'Happy Pair' is merely a maiden sweepstakes, and I hope I shall see Miss Kinseyle win a Derby yet in some London theatricals worthy of her powers."

"But, limiting eternity by the dressing-bell, Terra, even then I will not go on for ever. I'll join you in the gallery in three half seconds, if you'll get the piano open."

"But please observe," said Colonel Danby, "that if you go round that side of the table you will have to bury your sobs in the wrong sofa cushion, and then the whole effect will be spoiled. That's right; if you'll solemnly promise to keep the table on your right hand always, I will not torment you any more to-day."

"Don't mind my nonsense," said Edith. "I'm not a bit tired, really; and I am cultivating quite a taste for taking pains. But I must go now to Miss Fildare, for Sir James is sure to insist on that duet this evening, and she wants to get it up, I know."

The "Happy Pair" came first on the night of the performance, and Edith achieved a most triumphant *début*. The arrangements of the night were complete enough to give an air of reality even to the shower of bouquets with which the *débutante* was greeted, as she passed before the curtain in response to an enthusiastic call; and Colonel Danby gathered them up with graceful promptitude, placing the finest—which had been thrown by Sir James Margreave—in Edith's hands, while he bore the rest on her behalf.

"I am sure the flowers ought to be half yours," she said, when they got behind again. "I am entirely the product of your careful coaching."

"Not half mine," said the gallant Colonel. "This much of the bouquet"—drawing his finger round almost the whole of it, as he transferred the flowers he held himself to his left arm—"is due to your natural talents, and so much"—picking out a single rosebud from the edge—"is due to my teaching. May I keep my share?"

Edith smiled pleasantly at the compliment and the courteous grace of its delivery.

"With my grateful thanks—most certainly!"

"I dare say it will last longer than your share," he added, as he put it in his button-hole.

Some of the anxious performers who were to appear in the next piece were standing near them at the time, but, absorbed in their own affairs, paid no attention, and the two sat down on a sofa in the roomy wings, created for the occasion by a skilful adaptation of a conservatory to this purpose.

"But now," said the Colonel, getting up almost immediately, "I must prescribe for you. You will admit that I have not pressed you to take champagne till now. I do not approve of it to act upon, but after the nervous excitement of your triumph, it will be a sedative and not a stimulant."

He left her to go in search of the wine; and while she remained lying back in the corner of the sofa, a little tired, but thoroughly enjoying the pleasant flavour of the applause still ringing in her ears, one of the actors, ready dressed for the next piece, passed close in front of her. He was dressed as a gipsy, and so completely disguised that she did not immediately recognise beneath the black and red velvet and leather trimmings the true wearer—Count Garciola. Writing the following day to Mrs. Malcolm, and describing her impression, she said, after quickly and slightly sketching the events of the evening so far:

"And now I come to the important part of my story, because it has to do with something different from frivolous nonsense and passing amusements. I was resting, on a sofa behind the scenes after the play was over—left to myself for a few moments as it happened—when one of the actors came by ready dressed for his part, quite a disguise, a gipsy's dress, and I did not recognise him at once. But as I looked up, with my thoughts a hundred miles at the time from anything psychic, I saw him with some other sense besides eyesight, and it is most difficult to describe the thing to you just as it occurred. For an instant I thought his dress was smoking as if it was half on fire. He seemed to move along in the middle of a kind of pillar of cloud—nothing of a regular shape, but lumpy and massive round the upper part of him. But this moved with him, you understand, and was not left behind like smoke. It was dark in colour, with a lurid reddish glow, but irregular and patchy-—more dark in some places, and more red in others. I gazed in wonder, but he was not thinking of me, and took no notice. He passed in front of my sofa, and round by the end I was leaning on, and for a few moments he stood quite near me—within reach if I had put out my hand—for some one else came by behind me, and spoke to him in passing. As he stood in this way, the cloud round him wafted up against me, and then it gave me the strangest impressions. First of all a horrid thrill of feeling, something like what

I wrote to you about before, that made me suddenly turn almost faint, and *then*—it was just as though, when the cloud touched me, I suddenly saw *in it*, as in a kind of infinity that stretched all round me, an endless quivering mass of *tableaux vivants*, all mixed up together in the wildest confusion, but all of the same kind; all some sort of scene of violence in which the man in the middle of the cloud was engaged. For the moment I seemed to have his whole life whirling before me, and things it would take hours to tell seemed flashed upon me with such violence that my brain was all thrilling in a way I can't describe. It gave me the feeling, as it were, inside my head, that you have, don't you know, in a fast train when it suddenly dashes over an iron bridge, and the whirring uproar is distracting while it lasts. But I do not mean that I could now set to work and write down his biography. I could not do anything of the kind. But I have got the impression that I *have known*, though I have forgotten, everything, even down to details. All I can say, now, is that it is a horrible story. There are many women

mixed up in it, one in particular, whose image
flashed as it were out of a dozen corners at
once, and, since you commanded me, dear
Marian, so earnestly to tell you all my impressions, I will say that this woman seems
to be his wife. I don't mean to say that I
recognise Terra's features in the image—one
hasn't time to question an impression of that
sort before it is gone—but the idea that this
woman was, or was to be, his wife—for I
suppose I must look on all these dreadful
pictures as prophetic—was borne in on me as
if by a series of violent sledge-hammer blows,
if you understand what I mean, on the rafters
of the bridge, heard through the deafening
din as I dashed through. Of course you will
understand there was no noise really; it was
the racking thrill in my head that I am
wanting to indicate to you. For one instant
I can remember I seemed to see the woman
I am speaking of with a dagger in her hand,
and he grasping her wrist and throwing her
back on the ground. And then I can
remember instantaneous flashes of her seen
in tears and despair, or in fury, and half the
pictures I saw all the while seemed swimming

in blood. A few moments longer, I must have screamed or fainted; but suddenly all the sights around me seemed to shrink together again, and then I saw that the Count had passed on and was walking away —for the man in the gipsy dress, you will understand, was Count Garciola. It has given me such a feeling of horror for him that I can't bear the sight of him, and found myself manœuvring this morning to avoid the risk of possibly having to shake hands when I first met him at breakfast.

"I am fairly longing for a talk over the whole thing with you, and for a healthy refreshing bath of your good influence, dear Marian, after all this. I wonder if I could manage a day or two with you before Deerbury Park, after this visit is over. I should so much like it.

"And Colonel Danby, when he came back with some champagne he had been to fetch for me, thought my prostrate nervousness was all due to the excitement of the play. It was so ridiculous. I couldn't explain to him exactly what had happened, but I told him after a while that, though I had nearly fainted, it was not the play at all, but merely something in the nature of a ghost that I had seen—that I often saw such things, and that sometimes they made me uncomfortable. It made me laugh, the way he summed up my case, and put everything down to hallucinations conjured up by my highly-strung artistic temperament, and recommended riding, and lawn-tennis played earnestly, as the best preservatives from those sort of attacks in future."

Mrs. Malcolm telegraphed to Sidney Marston within ten minutes of reading this letter, and begged him to come over and consult with her that day if possible. The afternoon found him at her service in the drawing-room of her little Richmond villa, overlooking a sloping garden running down to the river. Mrs. Malcolm had no children, and lived by herself—when not visiting friends—in this quiet and graceful retreat, with a middle-aged man and his wife to look after her house, garden, and pony-carriage, and a couple of maids. She would sometimes have her brother to stay with her for a time—sometimes one of many feminine cousins—but just now she was by herself. Marston was soon put in possession of all the facts of the case.   As to the relations between Terra Fildare and Ferrars, he was acquainted with these already ; and now he was given Edith's letter to read, and asked for advice in the emergency.

" Is there any way of combating the frightful menace that seems hanging over that misguided girl, or do you take an impression like that to be fatally prophetic ?"

" I should be inclined," he said, " always to take a prophetic vision as a menace rather than as a fatality, constantly as we find such things verified by events.   It is one of the greatest mysteries how the future can be foreseen, when any future event is the product of a multiplicity of circumstances and independent acts by an indefinite number of people.   But, of course, future events are constantly being foreseen by clairvoyants, down to their smallest details, though the world at large, in its ignorance, prefers a lazy disbelief in the facts to the effort of attempting to account for them.   On the other hand, the prophetic vision may never do more than reveal the tendency of events as they stand at any given moment, and by the exercise of energy sufficient to control them they may be guided into a new channel."

After a little more vague metaphysical speculations on the subject, Marston threw out a new idea.

" But is it just possible that the vision or impression caught by Miss Kinseyle from this man's aura may not be prophetic at all, but strictly retrospective ?"

" How do you mean ?"

" Suppose the wife is not Miss Fildare in the future, but some other wife in the past ?"

" Ah, that is an idea ; but I never heard he had been married before. If he had been a widower he surely must have told Terra, and Lady Margreave would know, and I think she would have mentioned it to me."

" But suppose there might be no widower-hood in the matter ? It is merely a guess ; but suppose Count Garciola, who is clearly a reprobate, and is a wanderer about the world, has left a deserted wife somewhere in Spain or elsewhere ?"

Mrs. Malcolm gave vent to a low cry of apprehension and wonder.

"One has heard," Marston went on, " of such eccentricities as bigamy. The Count is likely to be a man of strong passions, and Miss Fildare, by all accounts, is a splendid prize."

" Poor infatuated girl !"

" It may be wrong to dwell on such a possibility without more evidence, but one could only get that—or stand a chance of getting it—through Miss Kinseyle's higher faculties properly awakened. If she comes to you, as she seems to think just possible, while the vision she has just had is still recent, it might be partially recovered in trance, and then examined more fully."

" I do wish she would come. If I can induce her ; of course, I shall try."

" Do you want," Marston asked after a pause, "to recover Miss Fildare for George ?'

" Why, the thought has never crossed my mind, because I have never supposed it possible. And there would be a long interval between even the realization of your terrible suspicion and the restoration of Terra to

George, which, indeed, is not the brightest dream I could have imagined, though I suppose it is useless to wish for anything better for him. His feelings are quite fixed—more's the pity."

She evidently spoke with more in her mind than she uttered, and Marston, without directly asking any question, waited silently, as though expecting further explanation.

" I had dreamed my dream on that subject," Mrs. Malcolm went on. " I hoped that George would have been drawn into the current of a new sympathy, and might have come to see how infinitely sweeter and nobler a companion for him Edith Kinscyle would have been. But I saw almost at once after they met that it was not to be—that he was too steadfast."

Marston still remained silent, and his features were set very rigidly as he gazed out across the garden, and between the trees which shaded it, to the gleam of the silver water beyond. A steam-launch puffed past the little opening of river visible as Mrs. Malcolm spoke, and emitted a discordant cry from its whistle.

"Do the boats annoy you much?" Marston said after a little while.

"The boats?" answered Mrs. Malcolm vaguely; "I hardly notice them. Yes," she went on after a little while, "that would have been a beautiful plan. It would have given George every prospect of happiness, and it would have linked Edith with myself, and perhaps with higher influences through me; but it is evidently not to be. To recover Terra might not render George really happy in the long run, but it is the only arrangement that will not involve him in certain unhappiness. How hard it is for the bits of colour in life's kaleidoscope to be rightly grouped! And if they are only a little wrong, how the picture is spoiled!"

"Indeed, that is so."

In the earnest depth of his utterance, the flavour of personal experience was but too perceptible.

"Who should know it better than yourself, Sidney?"

Mrs. Malcolm and her brother had known Marston from childhood, and the use of the

Christian name was natural to her when they were alone.

"Of course, my kaleidoscope has been fatally broken ; but that need not be talked of."

"Well, I need hardly say I grieve with you ; but, in one way, I look on you as like myself in reference to life. We neither of us live for it, but for something beyond. Of course, life is no good to you ; but then, for whom that truly realizes the future can it be of any good ? It can only be a matter of more or less patient waiting and performance of duty."

"We won't insult you by pushing the comparison too far. But the spirit in which you and I wait is very different, I fancy. It is one thing to wait, and merely feel dull ; and another thing to wait, enduring torture all the while."

"You are morbid. No blameless man like yourself should feel the shadow of another's sin like that."

"Another's sin ! I fear I am too cynical to feel that much ; but another's shame may dye one's own existence in every fibre."

Mrs. Malcolm only sighed, as over a problem for which she knew there was no solution.

CHAPTER XI.

Mrs. Malcolm had fretted with so keen a
sense of her own helplessness in the matter
against the circumstances which had threatened to keep Miss Kinseyle away from her
at this juncture, that she had trusted but
little to the hope Edith had expressed of
visiting her for a few days before she should
go to Deerbury Park. It was with as much
surprise as pleasure, therefore, that she
found this proposal suddenly take a definite
shape. Edith had not recurred to it again
in her letters, and only at the last moment,
about a week after the night of the theatricals, wrote to say that she would come to
Richmond for a few days if Mrs. Malcolm
would telegraph that she could receive her,
and would meet her, or have her met, by
such and such a train in London. The

answer had flashed back without a moment's loss of time, and George Ferrars—then in London wearing out a period of leave he had taken from his appointment at the Hague—was commissioned to meet the young lady at Euston Square and bring her on to Richmond. They arrived in comfortable time for dinner, to which feast Marston had also been summoned. Mrs. Malcolm and Edith had a little time to themselves in Edith's room beforehand.

"It is quite enchanting to be with you again, Marian," the girl declared. "And what a cosy nest you have here, with an exquisite view and sheltered privacy. What a pleasant room!"

"It is very good of you to have come, dear. Your feelers will have told you how much I wished it."

"It is very sweet of you to have wanted me; but for my part, I have had an under-current of longing to be here all the while I have been at Oatfield—charming as the visit has been. And that grew stronger, instead of waning with time. Only I was afraid Aunt Emma might raise insuperable objections. I diplomatised at last with exquisite skill — infected with Sir James's genius—and carried my point by surprise at a happy moment."

"In the great world, but not yet hopelessly and exclusively of it," Mrs. Malcolm said, with an affectionate caress.

"Not yet!—as if you had *almost* given me up for lost."

"You can't but be fought for by contending forces, my dear, and one or the other will conquer in the long run. Do you remember the vision I had of you at Compton Wood, as you balanced yourself on the fender ?"

"My own private tight-rope! I had quite forgotten."

"However, I don't see the least change in you. You are as—as natural and—well, I won't pay you compliments, I dare say you have had a surfeit of them—as much yourself as ever—your best self."

"And nowhere so much as with you—my real self—with nothing reserved and locked up in my inner nature, as has, of course, been always the case up there. And now I find you looking so well I have nothing more to ask after, for your brother has told me already that Mr. Marston is just as usual."

" He is coming here this evening."

" Capital! Then are you going to set to work upon me at once?"

" Are not the moments precious?"

" Ah! if life had fewer complications!" Edith sighed, acknowledging all that the question implied. " But tell me, now, have you been desperately disappointed in me? Because you expected some psychic justification for my visit to Oatfield, and I do not see that I have done more than form an extreme dislike for Count Garciola, and acquaint you with that mighty fact."

" My dear, I do not see how you could have done more, all by yourself. You have given us a clue. But now I must tell you some things to guard you against otherwise accidentally giving needless pain by talking of people at Oatfield. My poor brother George was in love with Terra Fildare, and she made the election you know of."

" Goodness! Did she know?"

"Certainly; and for a long while. That is all I need say. You will know now where the ice is thin."

They had a long gossip, and the little dinner party was so intimate as to put hardly any restraint on its continuance when they went downstairs. Edith met Mr. Marston with the frankest cordiality, and his manner was always so subdued and self-effacing, that his own gravity, and his silent observation of her as she talked, were in no way remarkable, nor suggestive of any abnormal emotions claiming especial restraint.

Mrs. Malcolm had given much thought to the problem how far to tell her brother what Edith had told her about her impressions of Count Garciola; but, unwilling on all grounds to shut George out from any mesmeric evenings they might have while Edith should be with her, she had decided finally that it was best to tell him all she had said, only suppressing the conjectures that had been built on the narrative by Mr. Marston. But their talk during dinner avoided the critical topic, and only touching lightly, while the servants were with them, on the incidents of their last meeting at Kinseyle Court, went off into the depths of mystic science generally, in connection with which Marston was drawn to talk, getting on to the vexed question of prophetic foresight in its various aspects, and the metaphysical theories which might be taken to reconcile the possibility of this with the sense each human being possessed, of power over his own acts. And then, after a while, he wound up hastily some remarks he was making, and apologised for talking up in the clouds about such comfortless abstractions.

"It seemed to *me*," said Edith, "that the conversation was just beginning to be really interesting. Please don't talk down to my level, Mr. Marston; I would much rather try and listen up to yours."

"Sidney is troubled from time to time, you know, Miss Kinseyle," said Ferrars, "with spasms of a modesty that is most exasperating. In another man it would merely be bidding for applause, but in him it is a mental affliction to be sympathised with. We are sorry for you, old man; but now you can go ahead again."

"It isn't a question of levels, in that sense," Marston said, with knitted brows and face a little bent down over his plate. "I think Miss Kinseyle knows pretty well where I think her natural level to be."

"But by that theory I have fallen sadly away from my proper place in the world. Would that be for my sins in some former condition of existence?"

"I don't see the signs of the falling away."

"But, look here, Mr. Marston, I am going to have this out with you once for all. I like to be thought well of, you know. I do not object to that at all; but I should almost better still like to be able to think well of myself. You may mean something that is very nice and pleasant for me, only I don't understand it in the least."

"What I mean is a conjecture—in some respects at all events—as to the form in which I put it; but I think it involves a great truth. Of course, in the case of each of us, this organism that we are working with, the body with all its thinking machinery, and so forth, is something different from *ourselves.* That, we are all agreed about, here, of course? No one would deny that, but the rankest materialist. But it is such a long idea to work out in conversation; it seems hardly——"

"He's having a relapse. Can't you administer something, Miss Kinseyle?"

"Go on, Mr. Marston, please. When I'm tired, I'll tell you to stop; and till I tell you you'll go on. Is that agreed?"

Veiled by the mock stateliness of her words and manner, a subtle compliment to his power of interesting her was embodied in this injunction, and made him look up with a pleasant smile. He went on addressing himself specially to her, and yielding more fully than before to the stimulating influence —the bright fascination—of her peculiar beauty.

"Well; what I come to next, working on from the plain fact that the body is an organism animated by the soul, is this: the body may be looked upon as a sort of instrument played upon by the soul—of course I use the word 'soul' in its poetical and not its technical occult sense."

" What is the technical occult sense ?" said Edith.

" An intermediate something between the body and the true spirit; but if you will let me put that aside for the moment, it will be better."

Edith nodded, and he went on :

" Well, if we grant that as a hypothesis, we come to what is clearly then a possibility —that, no matter how great a musician, so to speak, the soul may be, it cannot get more music out of the body than the quality of the instrument enables it to yield."

" I see. You mean, that we all feel possessed of grander ideas than we can express, of a higher nature than we can live up to ?"

" Not exactly that ; because anything we feel or think as definitely as that, is a tune played upon the instrument and within its capacity. The soul's thoughts on a higher level than the best capacities of the bodily brain, will not be susceptible of manifestation through that brain ; in other words, WE, in our ordinary waking state, can never be conscious of our own soul's highest thoughts—

though, certainly, impulses of feeling may reach the incarnate consciousness which are in a manner reflections of the higher state of consciousness; but that is a later complication of the idea."

"But if we are cut off from the best part of ourselves in that way, and from its thoughts, how are we to know anything about them, or know that we ever have such thoughts?"

"I think we may know, in the sense of being able to feel, by indirect methods quite sure, about the real state of the case. Firstly, we have the great method of mesmeric trance. It is constantly observed that clairvoyants of humble education and no great intelligence will talk, in the mesmeric state, up to a far higher level than they apparently belong to; and, in the same way, I think, every clairvoyante will, in the mesmeric state, in some way, transcend his or her natural or ordinary states."

"Even me," said Edith lightly, with the intonation that implied she was ranking herself low down on the scale.

"Even you," replied Marston, with a very

different intonation that gave the phrase the opposite meaning. " However fine the natural brain may be, as an instrument, the soul can think and perceive on a higher level, and, under the peculiar conditions of the mesmeric trance, reveal or record its perceptions by the lips of the sensitive. But there is another way of getting at the idea that the complete soul is a greater Being than the soul as it speaks through the body in ordinary waking life ; and that is the general review of what may be called the spiritual and psychological necessities of the case, if you think of the way in which the soul *must* really grow or evolve as time goes on."

Marston paused every now and then as he spoke ; but no one interrupted, and he could not misunderstand the general desire that he should develope his theory more fully.

" You see, it is nonsense, really," he said, " to think of the soul, incarnate in the body, as having taken its rise there. It is far too great a manifestation of the exalted potencies in Nature to be grown in that casual fashion. If it lives after the body, as we all feel quite sure it does, it certainly lived before also.

In other words, its real habitat or home is on the spiritual plane or planes of nature. Its manifestation in the body is, so to speak, a descent into that state of existence. Not necessarily an unimportant process, or an accidental collapse of its higher attributes; not a fall, but a descent with a purpose: a descent in search of fresh experience, of fresh energy—as typified by the classical fable. Now, I should be disposed to regard that descent as the growth by the soul through its contact with matter—of the body, it developes in each case—which we are often too much in the habit of regarding as *the person*, complete as we see it. But it does not in the least degree follow that we should necessarily suppose that the whole soul—if I may use that expression—subsides into the body each time it attaches itself to a body, and partially transfers its consciousness to that body. It is a difficult idea to realize, because each person feels to be a complete entity in himself. But still it is very comprehensible that the centre of consciousness, which is impressed with that feeling, might, when transferred to another plane of nature, wake up to the use of a host of new faculties, and thus find its consciousness immensely expanded, without being any the less conscious of identity with itself as formerly functioning in the body."

" It's *perfectly* intelligible," Edith declared. " Don't you think so, Marian ?"

Mrs. Malcolm indicated assent.

"But now tell me," Edith asked, " how this bears on what we began by talking about — when we were speaking of our various levels ?"

" I suppose," said Mrs. Malcolm, as Marston hesitated a little before framing his answer, "that he means your spiritual portion—your Higher Self, may be on a very high level."

" The ' Higher Self' is a very good expression," said Marston ; " as bringing what I mean to a focus. I think, after the little observation we have had of you, even in the mesmeric state, that we may recognise your Higher Self as being undeniably on a very exalted level."

" Then why should it have such an inferior body ?"

She put the question with perfect simplicity, following out the train of thought Marston had suggested, but the turn of the phrase naturally raised a laugh, and Ferrars protested :

" Miss Kinseyle, I protest, as an admiring friend of your lower self, which is quite good enough 'for the likes of me,' against the rudeness with which you speak of it from the heights of your Higher Self. I wonder what sort of a body *would* content you ?"

Marston did not venture on turning the opening afforded to the service of a compliment, and merely said, still keeping to the serious and philosophical vein :

" Relatively to the Higher Self, of course, any physical organism must necessarily be imperfect. There are questions that may be more easily asked than answered about these mysteries; but I can imagine that a very highly developed entity or soul may sometimes descend into incarnation—or grow a body — whichever way we like to put it, under the dictate of some specific and limited necessity. You may, for instance, have already gained, and have passed into the permanent essence of your being, much that I am now only labouring to acquire. The organism you have now developed may not have been required to seek experience in that direction. But remember this is little more than guess-work."

" At any rate, Mr. Marston," said Edith, " it is a beautiful, beautiful theory, even if the least satisfactory part of it is the last part—required to make me out a more wonderful person than I seem. Oh, goodness! what a contrast it is to be talking about such things after our frivolities at Oatfield ?"

This led to some questions about the theatricals ; but Edith fenced these, and declared that after talking about her highest, she could not drop suddenly down to her lowest self.

" Let me keep, at any rate, on the intermediate level in which I can listen to Mr. Marston. And I do not remember, Mr. Marston," she added, with the resumption of her mock queenliness, " that I ever gave you leave to stop; so you will please continue."

"I had finished; and I think it was time after such a lecture. With your permission, my next performance will be to get you to talk—in the way you talked at Kinseyle Court."

"I'm quite ready—whenever you choose." said Edith.

They had all dined lightly, but still it was decided they should wait a little while before attempting any mesmerism, so the ladies went first into the drawing-room, while Ferrars and his friend had a cigar. They were well aware that it would be no compliment to Mrs. Malcolm to refrain, as she was known by both to look with a calm but emphatic scornfulness upon the affectations which in some ladies' houses condemned gentlemen guests to privations in this respect. A few words on this subject led Ferrars to add:

"Yes; Marian has no littlenesses. There are very few women like her."

"She is strong and grand: such a splendid friend for Miss Kinseyle to lean upon."

"You trust Miss Kinseyle's psychic faculties, don't you?" Ferrars asked, after a little pause.

"I'm sure they are of a very fine order. But we have got to be sure we read their observations aright."

"Marian has told me of some impressions she has had while staying with the Margreaves. What do you make of all that?"

"I don't think we have ground to feel sure yet that we can read those suspicions aright. They seem to foreshadow trouble. Whether we can enable Miss Kinseyle to present them to us in a more defined way, so that they may possibly serve as warnings for the person chiefly concerned, remains to be seen."

"The worst of all this is that such warnings can hardly ever reach the person chiefly concerned, and would not be likely to secure much attention if they did; especially if they seemed to come in any way through myself, they could only be misinterpreted."

Marston did not press any contrary view of the matter on his friend. They talked on, round about the subject for awhile.

Ferrars was not, so far, inclined to regard

the statements Miss Kinseyle had made as having any practical bearing on his own great disappointment; and his interest in the proceedings was not really very keen when they eventually settled down, in the drawing-room, to the undertaking Mrs. Malcolm and Marston had in view.

Miss Kinseyle lay back in comfort in the corner of a sofa, Marston sat beside her, and the lights were a little subdued and so arranged that none should shine directly on her face.

" It gives me such a pleasant, comfortable feeling—drowsy, but not in the least faint," Edith said, as he took her hands to hold for a little while before attempting to bring on the trance. " Don't hurry me off too soon !"

"We will be as deliberate as you please. Only let us make a bargain that you will not be too obstinate in refusing to come back to us after you have been long enough away."

" Whatever does my poor little obstinacy in the matter signify, when you can pull me back, *nolens volens*, whenever you choose—

just as if I was a butterfly at the end of a string."

" I certainly would not be instrumental in sending you off for a flight unless I felt sure that I could bring you back."

" When I am further advanced, perhaps, I shall develope a will of my own, and come and go as I choose. Just fancy, you all waiting patient and helpless till to-morrow morning while I should be amusing myself in another world, and forgetting all about you. Oh, by-the-bye, you will not forget to make me remember this time, will you ?"

" Everything of importance. I do not suppose you will be able yet to remember everything, but I will try to impress you to remember the best things. I am not in a hurry," he added, as he began gently stroking her forehead. " You shall only go off gradually."

" It is such a strong influence. Good-bye, Marian. I'll remember to give her your love. Will you remind me if I should forget," she said with a smile, looking up at Marston.

He nodded without speaking, and then. as he drew down both hands slowly close to her face, her eyes closed, and she remained quite still, giving a gentle little sigh of contentment. Marston went on silently, making passes over her face and head, and presently she laughed, and her face broke into a smile, though with the eyes still shut.

"Tell me what amuses you," Marston said.

"Is she gone off, then?" said Ferrars *sotto voce* to her sister.

The laugh had not suggested the idea, but her answer to Marston confirmed it.

"The little man in green made me laugh; he looks so funny, all changing colours as he bows to me. Now he's blue."

"Ask him if he can give you any information about your recent visions."

"He says he can try to find out anything I want to know. But—what?——" Then she laughed again. "I can't."

"Can't do what," asked Marston.

"Slip about in the way he does. He's here, there, and everywhere at once."

"Ask him if he knows your Spirit Queen."

" He says he will find out anybody I want him to find out."

" Well, say you will give him a trial. Ask him to find out Count Garciola."

Edith gave a little shudder, and her expression darkened. Then in a few moments it changed again, and she moved her head slightly on her pillow and murmured :

" Yes ; that will be better."

" What will be better ?"

" He will show me the way to where the Spirit Queen is—— Oh, it was you."

" What was it he did ?"

" It was he took me there before, he says, though I did not see him then. I remember there was some one with me as I went."

" That will be very nice presently, tell him ; but you must insist on getting him first to tell you what you want to know about Count Garciola."

" He says I know all about it if I will only remember. Yes ; so I do ; that's true, but what a disagreeable subject. What— were you with me then too ? Why, you go about everywhere." Again she smiled. " He says, Why not. It's easy to go about. The hard thing is to keep still."

Marston patiently resumed his efforts to keep her attention fixed upon the questions he wished answered.

" But ask your new friend to remind you what it was you saw about that woman Count Garciola was treating badly."

" What woman ?—oh, I remember, his wife. She tried to kill him. Horrible people, all of them. It was on account of the other woman, but he drove her away, and she is in great distress now."

" Now !" said Ferrars, in a whisper to his sister, looking at her in bewilderment ; " what does it mean ?"

" Hush !" Mrs. Malcolm whispered back. " Don't speak ; listen, but control your *feelings* even, for the present, or you may disturb her."

" Are you talking," asked Marston, " of something that is going to happen in the future, or of something that has happened already ?"

Edith looked restless and perplexed.

" I see it all before me as if it was happening now," she said.

" Where is it happening?"

" Where—I don't know. What—where's he gone?"

" Has your new friend gone away?"

" Yes."

" Wish him to come back."

" Oh, he'll be back directly, I am sure. He's gone to find out something. There! there he is like a flash again. How funny!"

" What is funny?"

" I don't know. He seemed to be so full of the idea, he splashed it over me."

" What idea?"

" Seville—the woman he deserted is in Seville."

" You mean his wife by the woman he deserted."

" His wife that wanted to kill him. Yes. But it makes me feel so uncomfortable. Let me go away."

Marston looked round at his companions. Both looked pale and excited.

" We mustn't force her," Marston said,

holding her hand, and resting his other hand on her forehead. "Have you had enough?"

"Some further detail, for Heaven's sake," said Ferrars.

"Directly," Marston said to the clairvoyante in an earnest soothing voice. "Only one more question, and then we will be off elsewhere. Ask your friend to tell you some name by means of which we can find the woman in Seville."

" I don't think he wants to go again."

" Remember it is to do good that we want to know this. Try and bear the discomfort a little longer for Marian's sake. She wants to know so badly. And tell your friend you wish him to find out the name the woman bears. Is she known as Countess Garciola?"

" No," Edith said presently in a laboured voice. " He's gone; he'll be back soon. I'm bearing it for Marian's sake; but it makes me feel giddy and afraid to stand still and alone like this. What *nasty* things!"

" Don't look at them; order them to be gone. You are mistress, remember, and they must remember it too. The country is pretty where you are, isn't it?"

" Ah! there he is again, Bernaldez! That's the name of the woman, though it's false. It's over the shop quite plain. I see it in a square, with a fountain near. *Don't* hold me any longer."

"There, now you can go on, and your friend will show you the way. Off you go!"

" Phew—what a relief! That's delightful."

" Tell me something of what you see as you go along. You must not forget us at this end of the line altogether, you know."

" I can see the line all right; and bright mountains all about, cheerful and pleasant. He draws me along like a feather."

" Hasn't he got a name, your new friend?"

" A name? what is his name? Any name will do for him, he says; I can call him Zephyr if I like."

" Very well. Now you will remember Zephyr when you come back, won't you, and what he looks like?"

" There he is changing colours and shapes again for fun; but I'll remember. But where are we? this is not the same place as before.

But oh—h! there SHE is again; and what does anything matter!"

" Now look at her earnestly, and remember her appearance above all things, and anything she says to you. Think as she speaks to you that you will treasure up her words."

" Yes, yes—I shall never forget her. My Queen, it is heaven to be with you. I'll never be faithless to her. No, never, never! how could I be ?"

These disjointed exclamations were murmured slowly, with little intervals between each, in a tone of rapt adoration.

Her words gradually subsided into an only half-articulate utterance, though she spoke with no apparent sense of effort, and the confusion of what she said seemed merely to reflect the vagueness of the blissful emotion she experienced. For a time Marston remained silent.

" She cannot come to harm," he said to Mrs. Malcolm in a low aside, " in such care as that. Such a bath of spiritual glory must be a blessing to her. Do you see or feel anything ?"

" I feel *her* influence strongly ; but I see

nothing. I suppose I am too much excited about the other matter."

" Don't think of that just yet, or it may disturb her."

Edith remained silent now and very still, her face, as it were, glowing with the emotion working through her innermost nature. At last Marston said, speaking gently, as he bent down by her side, but distinctly :

" Is she the same as the Countess ?"

" Yes," whispered Edith softly after a short pause. " She is the same as the Countess ; but I belong to her too. You know how it is," she says. " I am to trust to your intuition to explain it ; and I may trust you entirely to lead me right."

She moved her hand, as it lay on her lap, towards Marston as she spoke. He made no reply, though he took the hand ; but bent down his head, turning a little away from her, as though struggling with an emotion that he could hardly master.

" Tell her to remember that," whispered Mrs. Malcolm behind him ; but he shook his head.

" No, no ; I must use no psychic influence

in that way ; it must be as she chooses. She will always command my whole soul's loyalty and devotion to be spent to its last throb in her service."

The last words were in too low a whisper to be heard distinctly by the others, and were breathed rather to Edith herself than uttered aloud.

"How you are dragging at the thread," said Edith restlessly.

Marston sat up erect in his chair, and passed his hand once or twice over her head and face.

"Rest quietly with your Higher Self, till she in her wisdom sends you back. Give me a sign when it is time for you to return, and trust me to take care of the thread."

END OF VOL. I.

BILLING & SONS, PRINTERS, GUILDFORD